Assassins
–in the–
Cathedral

Trailblazer Books

Also by Dave and Neta Jackson

Hero Tales: A Family Treasury of True Stories
From the Lives of Christian Heroes (Volumes I, II, & III)

Assassins
–in the–
Cathedral

Dave & Neta Jackson

Story Illustrations by
Julian Jackson

BETHANY HOUSE PUBLISHERS
MINNEAPOLIS, MINNESOTA 55438

Assassins in the Cathedral
Copyright © 1999
Dave and Neta Jackson

Illustrations © 1999
Bethany House Publishers

Story illustrations by Julian Jackson.
Cover design and illustration by Catherine Reishus McLaughlin.

Scripture quotations are from the King James Version of the Bible.

Published by Bethany House Publishers
A Ministry of Bethany Fellowship International
11400 Hampshire Avenue South
Minneapolis, Minnesota 55438
www.bethanyhouse.com

Printed in the United States of America by
Bethany Press International, Minneapolis, Minnesota 55438

ISBN 0–7642–2012–8

All the background events and many of the people in this story whose names are publicly known are historically true. The reign of terror by General Idi Amin; the worldwide ministry of evangelist Festo Kivengere; Archbishop Janini Luwum's arrest and death; a play reenacting the story of the early martyrs for the Church of Uganda's Centennial; the disappearance of six young actors . . . all are true.

However, the Kabaza family (Theo, Eunika, Faisi, Yacobo, and Blasio), their relationship to Bishop Kivengere, and their involvement in Archbishop Luwum's household are fictional. We tell the story through their eyes only to help tell the other events and their impact on ordinary Christians like the Kabaza family. In this way we hope to protect the privacy of the *real* parents, probably still living, of the six young actors who suffered the terrible events in the spring of 1977, Kampala, Uganda.

Special thanks to Jackie Nalule and her family from Uganda, who gave us invaluable help about Ugandan life and culture. Any inaccuracies are our fault alone.

DAVE AND NETA JACKSON are a husband/wife writing team who have authored and coauthored many books on marriage and family, the church, and relationships, including the books accompanying the Secret Adventures video series, the Pet Parables series, the Caring Parent series, and the newly released *Hero Tales,* volumes I, II, and III.

The Jacksons have two married children: Julian, the illustrator for TRAILBLAZER BOOKS, and Rachel, who has recently blessed them with a granddaughter, Havah Noelle. Dave and Neta make their home in Evanston, Illinois.

CONTENTS

Chapter 1

The Good Friday Parade

Y ACOBO KABAZA PUSHED HIS WAY through the crowd that was slowly winding its way like a lazy snake through the streets of Kabale. The fourteen-year-old looked this way and that in growing frustration. It was just like his little brother to disappear in the middle of the Good Friday parade! Always goofing off—even on a solemn occasion like today! And where was he supposed to look for him? Yacobo didn't know whether ten-year-old Blasio had dropped back to be with some of his friends or had run ahead.

Yacobo did know one thing: His mother would give him a piece of her mind if he showed up back at the house without Blasio. Why did he always get stuck looking after his little brother? Yacobo hadn't even wanted to come to the parade today; he'd wanted to stay home and work on the ending of the story he was writing. After all, if he got the story finished, he could show it to Bishop Kivengere when the bishop and his wife came over to see his parents this evening.

But, no, the whole family had to come to the parade, and he was supposed to keep track of Blasio.

"This is important, Yacobo," his mother had said firmly. "We promised Bishop Kivengere we would all be at the parade again this year as a witness of Christian unity."

Bishop Festo Kivengere sure wasn't afraid to speak his mind, Yacobo thought with grudging admiration as he pushed and shoved his way through the parade marchers, trying to keep an eye out for Blasio. The dynamic evangelist was the Anglican bishop of the Kigezi district, nestled in the southwestern corner of Uganda in East Africa. His sermons in St. Peter's Cathedral here in Kabale, the largest town in the district, tended to be unforgettable.

"If Christ tells us to love even our enemies," the bishop had preached two years ago, *"how can we have hatred in our hearts for fellow Christians? There is already too much political violence and tribal hatred in Uganda today. What must the Muslims and unbelievers think when they see us Christians fighting about our differences? Only the love of Christ— for one another and for our enemies—can overcome the violence and divisions in our land."*

That woke people up! So here they were on Good Friday, 1976, joining hands with Kabale's Catholics for only the second time in Uganda's history. As it had turned out, the people who were most affected by last year's parade were the Protestants and Catholics who had marched in it. Yacobo had been startled when both his father and mother had confessed wrong attitudes in their hearts and asked forgiveness of their Catholic neighbors. They were eager to march in the parade again this year.

But not Yacobo. If he didn't get back home soon, he'd never get his story done in time to give it to the bishop that evening. And now Blasio was missing!

For weeks Yacobo had been writing a story for English class at Kigezi High School—a story he wanted to show Bishop Kivengere because it was partly about him. Once Yacobo had started writing, the story seemed to grow on him like a second skin. Walking to and from school, in bed at night, sometimes even when his mother was talking to him!—the story kept turning over and over in his mind. Even now, halfheartedly looking for Blasio among the parade marchers, Yacobo kept thinking of ways to write the final paragraphs. Should he stop when the firing squad fired their rifles? Or should he—

"Eh! Yacobo! You should see the big cross and gold statues they're carrying at the front of the parade!" a voice giggled at his elbow. "And the Catholic fellow walking with Bishop Kivengere sure is wearing a funny hat!"

"Blasio!" Yacobo snapped, grabbing his little

brother's arm. "Didn't Mama tell you to stay with me during the parade?"

Blasio's mischievous grin faded. "No," he pouted, jerking his arm away. "She told *you* to stick with *me*. Besides, I came back, didn't I?"

Yacobo pressed his lips tightly together. If he told Mama that Blasio had run off, she would probably be upset with *him* for not keeping a sharp eye on his little brother—and then there would be a big upset. It would probably be best to say nothing.

To Yacobo's relief, Blasio didn't say anything, either, when they got home. It would have been just one more worry for their parents. Their beloved country, Uganda, "the pearl of Africa," seemed on the brink of ruin after six years of President Idi Amin's terrorist rule. And now they'd heard rumors about violence at Makerere University, where Yacobo's older sister, Faisi, was a first-year student. Just rumors so far—nothing on the radio or in the newspapers. But Kampala, the capital of Uganda, where the university was, was only 260 miles from Kabale, and news had a way of trickling to the outlying towns.

It was these rumors that had prompted Yacobo's parents to invite Bishop Kivengere and his wife to come and pray with them for Faisi's safety that evening after the Good Friday parade. Tea was at six; that meant he still had three hours till they arrived, Yacobo thought gratefully, slipping out into the tiny garden in back of the house with the notebook that contained his story. It was the only place he had any real privacy.

He opened the notebook and skimmed back over what he'd already written. The story was about three young men who had been executed by Idi Amin's soldiers right here in Kabale's stadium four years earlier when Yacobo was only ten years old. Bishop Kivengere had been there; the Kabaza family had been there—they knew the families of the three young men who had faced the firing squad. Yacobo had not really understood what crime the three young men had committed. But two years after General Idi Amin had staged a military coup and named himself "President for Life" of Uganda, the young men had been accused of treason and ordered to be killed in a public execution as a warning to others. There had been no trial. Just accusations, the arrests . . . then the firing squad.

Yacobo hadn't wanted to go to the stadium. How terrible to go see people be executed! But Eunika Kabaza, his mother, had said, *We can't let those young men die alone with no one to be their witnesses! I could never face their parents again!*

And so they had gone to the stadium that day with three thousand other Kabale residents. The crowd was silent and grieving. It should have been a terrible day—except for the strange and wonderful thing that had happened. Bishop Kivengere had asked for permission from the army captain in charge to speak with the prisoners before the execution. But as the bishop stepped forward to speak to the condemned men, all three had turned to face him with smiles of joy. "Oh, bishop!" one cried. "The day I was arrested, in my cell, I asked the Lord Jesus to come into my heart. Tell my wife not to worry. I am going to heaven to be with Jesus!"

The other two told similar stories, raising their handcuffed hands upward in praise. The youngest one said, "Please warn my younger brothers never to go away from the Lord Jesus!"

Moments later shots rang out, and all three fell to the ground.

Everyone was stunned. Most of the witnesses had not been able to hear what the prisoners had said to Bishop Kivengere; they could only see the smiling faces and hear the joyful shouts. What had happened to make them so unafraid? Later, preaching at St. Peter's Cathedral, Bishop Kivengere had told their story as they'd related it in the few moments before they died. What Idi Amin had meant for evil, God had used for good.

It was a powerful story—but Yacobo worried whether he had written it well enough. Had he shown what it felt like for a ten-year-old boy to stand in the stadium under the warm East African sun, waiting for three young men barely in their twenties to die by firing squad? Could the reader *feel* his amazement when the young men—

"Welcome! Welcome!" His father's voice from inside the house broke into Yacobo's thoughts. Bishop

Kivengere and his wife, Mera, must have arrived. Yacobo closed the notebook carefully. It would have to do. He slipped into the house, where his father, Theo Kabaza, was escorting their guests to the table in the small room that was used for both sitting and eating. Theo Kabaza was a tall, sturdy man who looked more like a farmer or cattleman than a city taxi driver, though he'd driven a taxi as long as Yacobo could remember. "We are so concerned about Faisi at the university," he said. "We don't know what to believe about the rumors we hear."

Yacobo sat on the floor near the four adults and glared a warning at his brother, not wanting Blasio's usual antics to get them sent outside. He carefully held the notebook containing his story, waiting for a chance to show it to the bishop. But not yet . . .

Eunika Kabaza offered milk and sugar to go with the tea and passed plates of bread and butter. "Have you heard anything from Charity about that Kenyan girl who disappeared?" she asked anxiously. Charity Kivengere, Festo and Mera's youngest daughter, was also a student at the university.

Festo Kivengere shook his head. He was not a large man, but his outgoing personality and warm nature seemed to fill the room. "Not from Charity, no," he said. "She doesn't want to worry us. But I'm afraid some of the rumors are true. The Kenyan student was trying to get out of the country, was stopped for questioning at the airport, and has simply disappeared. And, unfortunately, just last week we heard that another student was shot by soldiers off campus."

Yacobo saw the look of alarm on his mother's face.

"But"—the bishop held up his hands soothingly—"that doesn't mean the students are in danger. We don't know why the Kenyan girl was arrested, but the Kenyan government has been very critical of President Amin recently, and so the president may be playing some kind of political game. As for the shooting, we don't know if it was political or just a drunken brawl with police."

"Oh, we never should have let Faisi go to the university," said Yacobo's mother, wringing her hands.

Mera Kivengere laid her hand on the other woman's arm. "Sister Eunika, doesn't Faisi's name mean 'faith'? You must trust our Lord to care for your daughter. We cannot hide our children beneath our skirts forever." Her voice was gentle, but it had strength in it. Years ago she and Festo had lost a daughter to a childhood illness.

"Yes," the bishop agreed, "we, too, are concerned. But Faisi and Charity are brilliant young women. If our country is ever to come out of these dark days, our children must be educated and prepared to function in the worldwide community. If we give up, we have already let Idi Amin win his war of destruction."

The four adults continued to talk, sharing verses of comfort from the Bible, and then the praying began. Yacobo's mother cried, and the bishop prayed for God's peace to replace "the spirit of fear." Then they prayed some more.

Yacobo squirmed. If the bishop thought his sister was all right, that was good enough for him. How long was this prayer meeting going to go on?

Suddenly the Kivengeres were rising and saying they must be going. Yacobo leaped to his feet.

"B-bishop—sir," he stuttered. "May I speak to you?" He dropped to his knees in the traditional

17

Ugandan greeting of respect.

"Yacobo!" said Festo Kivengere warmly. "You boys were so quiet, I forgot you were here. How is school going? You started high school this year, am I right? And keeping up with your studies, I hope!"

Festo Kivengere had been a teacher for twenty years, while preaching and going on evangelistic missions in the evenings, on weekends, and on school holidays. He always asked Yacobo about his studies.

"Oh yes, sir!" said Yacobo. "In fact, that's what I wanted to talk to you about." He thrust the notebook into Bishop Kivengere's hands. "I . . . I've written a story for English class, and I wondered if you would read it and give me your opinion. Because—well, I'd like to be a writer someday, and I wonder if you think . . . well . . ." Yacobo didn't know what to say next.

"Yacobo, the bishop is a busy man," scolded his father. "He doesn't have time to correct school papers anymore. Festo, I apologize for my son—"

"No, no, it's all right," said the bishop graciously. "I will read it when I get a chance and let you know what I think. All right?" He smiled at Yacobo, bid Theo, Eunika, and Blasio good-night, and walked with his wife into the sweet springtime evening with Yacobo's story under his arm.

The messenger arrived just as the Kabazas were sitting down to their dinner after the joyous Easter worship service at St. Peter's Cathedral two days later.

"Bishop Kivengere asks if we can come to their home for tea this evening," said Yacobo's father, reading the message. He looked up at his wife. "All of us—the whole family."

Eunika's eyes widened. "Do . . . do you think it's bad news? Maybe he has heard something from the university! Oh, Theo—"

"Now, Eunika, have you forgotten how we prayed the other night? Faisi is in God's hands. We must trust in Him. Let's eat this excellent *luwombo* you have prepared"—Theo eyed the steaming bowl of green bananas boiled and mashed in banana leaves, as well as the fried beef and *lumonde,* or boiled sweet potatoes, and rubbed his hands together—"and then we will pay a visit to the Kivengeres."

A few hours later Theo drove the family in his taxi through the empty streets of Kabale and pulled up at the bishop's home. Festo Kivengere greeted them wearing a casual shirt and slacks. It was one of the few times Yacobo had seen him without his clergy collar and black suit coat.

"I will come right to the point," said the bishop when they were seated and Mera was serving the tea. "I read Yacobo's story yesterday, and one thing is very clear to me—this boy has great potential to be a talented writer. He should be given the best education possible to prepare him for university. There is a school in Kampala that has a strong writing program for students his age and—"

"Festo!" cried Eunika. "What are you saying? It is hard enough to let Faisi go so far away to school, especially to the capital, where there is so much violence these days. But like you have said, she is almost a grown woman. But Yacobo is only fourteen, and I could never . . ."

Yacobo's ears were burning. Had he heard right? The bishop had said, *"This boy has great potential to be a talented writer."* A talented writer!

"Let me finish, dear Eunika," said the bishop. "I know your concern. But as I was thinking and praying about this, I remembered that Archbishop Janini Luwum in Kampala has asked me to recommend some trustworthy people for his household staff. Theo, you used to drive taxi in Kampala for a few years, did you not? And, Eunika, you are not only a worthy woman of God, but you also are an excellent cook. I know! Every time we break bread at your house, I have to go on a diet!" Festo laughed and patted his stomach. Then he got serious again. "The archbishop needs a cook and a personal driver. Would you consider making such a change—your whole family? That way Yacobo could begin his education in earnest and you would be able to see Faisi frequently and satisfy your concern that she is all right. What do you say?"

A stunned silence filled the bishop's sitting room as Theo and Eunika looked with round eyes and open mouths at Festo and Mera.

Yacobo heard all the words the bishop had said, but only one phrase stuck in his head: *great potential to be a talented writer . . . great potential to be a talented writer . . .*

Chapter 2

The Hijacked Airliner

ARCHBISHOP JANINI LUWUM and his wife, Mary, were pleased with Festo Kivengere's recommendation of the Kabazas for their household staff. By the time the boys' schools let out for summer holiday in early April, the plan was settled. The Kabazas sold their small house, packed up their belongings, and set out in Theo's taxi for Kampala.

It was Uganda's rainy season, and the squeaky windshield wipers kept up a steady beat mile after mile. The car seemed to crawl along the wet, tarred road, which had turned muddy red from the rich red earth along its shoulders.

Twice they were stopped at roadblocks by soldiers who demanded to know who they were, where they were going, and why. The boys watched, wide-eyed, as Theo got out of the car and stood in the rain while the soldiers looked at the letter from the archbishop. Both times they were finally waved on.

Yacobo had never been to Uganda's capital city. From a distance he could see tall, modern buildings and red-tiled roofs nestled among Kampala's seven hills. But as the taxi threaded its way through the city's nearly deserted streets late that evening, he saw soldiers on many street corners, stores boarded up, and windows and walls pock-marked with bullet holes—grim reminders of Uganda's ongoing civil war.

The taxi climbed Namirembe Hill, and the boys stared as St. Paul's Church—Namirembe Cathedral—loomed into view. "The Protestant church in Uganda will be celebrating its Centennial next year," Theo told his sons as they passed the beautiful cathedral.

"What's centennial?" Blasio asked.

"It means a hundred years, empty-headed boy," Yacobo muttered.

"That's right," their father said. "One hundred years ago the first Protestant missionaries came to Uganda and presented the Gospel to King Kabaka Mutesa. He was eager to know more, but his Muslim son, Kabaka Mwanga, who later became king, hated Christianity and killed three of his own servant boys who had become Christians."

"Boys?" said Blasio in disbelief.

"Theo . . ." cautioned Eunika, frowning.

But Theo was enjoying his role of teacher. "That's right. They were the first Ugandan Christian martyrs."

Yacobo was silent. Uganda's tribal kingdoms were supposedly united under a president now. But from the little he knew about the former president, Milton Obote, and the current president, Idi Amin, presidents weren't much improvement over kings. If the president didn't like you, you died.

The taxi slowed, then turned into a large, open gate. The archbishop's residence was large and roomy without being lavish or showy. Even though it was late, the Kabazas were welcomed graciously by Mrs. Luwum and shown to the staff living quarters behind the house. They had a few days to get settled and get the boys enrolled in school before Theo and Eunika started their new duties as driver and cook.

"Oh, Theo, let's go see Faisi at the university tomorrow," Eunika said after the car was unloaded. "I just want to know that she's all right."

Faisi Kabaza poked her brothers playfully as she led her family down the hall to her student room on the campus of Makerere University. "Boys aren't usually allowed in the women's residence hall, you know," she teased. "But since you're family . . ."

Faisi was petite, like her mother. She had dancing brown eyes and a lilting voice. She spoke excellent English and already seemed so much more wise and grown-up in Yacobo's eyes.

He tried to look interested as the family crowded into his sister's room. The room was small and shared by several other young women. Bunk beds and chests of drawers seemed to fill every inch of space. He wondered if the men's residence hall was like this one. Where could a person study in such a small, crowded room?

"So what's it like living at the archbishop's residence?" Faisi asked.

"A lot bigger than this!" Blasio piped up.

Faisi laughed. "And Bishop Kivengere really thinks you have writing talent?" she said, eyeing Yacobo in a half-mocking, half-admiring way.

Yacobo blushed. He was just going to tell his sister what the bishop had said when Blasio crowed, "Hey, Faisi, look at me!" The ten-year-old had put both feet in a wastebasket and was hopping around the small room like a one-legged toad.

"Blasio!" scolded Eunika, impatiently hauling her youngest son out of the wastebasket.

Yacobo rolled his eyes. They should have left this clown back at the archbishop's house. "Where do you study?" he asked his sister, trying to sound grown-up and serious.

"At the library," she said. "Come on, I'll show you."

"Uh, maybe another time," said Theo Kabaza quickly. He looked uncomfortable in his suit and tie. "Are you sure you're all right, Faisi? We heard that there have been demonstrations on campus against the government—you know, after that Kenyan girl disappeared and the other student was killed. Why don't you come live with us for this next school term? At least until things settle down and are safe again."

Faisi looked upset. "No, please, Papa. I don't want to interrupt my studies. I've only just started! Don't worry; I'll be fine. I'm not political. I just mind my own business and do my schoolwork."

Theo and Eunika looked at each other. "All right," Theo sighed. "But . . . please be careful."

Yacobo was disappointed not to see the library. He'd read practically all the books in his school library back in Kabale and would love to see a really big library. But surely they would visit Faisi again soon.

Yacobo had not seen Festo Kivengere since they'd moved to Kampala. His parents said the Kivengeres were traveling in Europe for a series of evangelistic meetings. At a youth convention in Germany, Festo was scheduled to share the preaching with his friend Billy Graham, the American evangelist.

But before he left Uganda, the bishop had put in a good word for Yacobo at the Senior School for Arts and Science, and Yacobo had been placed in an advanced writing class, even if he was only a Senior 1 student.

Once the school term started again in June, Yacobo settled into a familiar routine. Dressed in his school uniform—white shirt, khaki shorts, and gray knee socks with a red band around the top—he quickly ate his breakfast of millet boiled into a mush and walked Blasio to his primary school. Then he caught a *matatus,* a small bus that took him to the senior school. Yacobo got out of school later than Blasio, so his mother usually picked up his little brother in the afternoon.

Yacobo felt strange at first in his new school. Back at Kigezi High School, many of the students—like himself—were from the Bahororo tribe, and they spoke the familiar Ruhororo language on the playground. School classes were taught in English, and most students also had to study Swahili, Africa's trade language. But here in Kampala, the students came from many different tribal backgrounds—Kakwa, Langi, Acholi, Iteso, Banyankole, and others—and each one had its own dialect. So even on the playground the students had to use English.

It was also the first time Yacobo realized that a person's tribal background could get him in trouble.

During his first week at the new school, one of the Senior 4 boys backed him up against a wall and looked him up and down. "Your name—Yacobo—is that a Christian name?" the boy demanded.

Slowly Yacobo nodded. Like many Christian parents in Uganda, his parents had christened him with a name from the Bible: Jacob, or Yacobo.

"You're Langi, then? Or Acholi?"

Yacobo shook his head. "Bahororo. Does it matter?"

The boy sneered. "You're lucky you're not Langi. Langi are traitors. *Ex*-President Obote was Langi." He put a lot of emphasis on "ex."

The older boy started to walk away. But Yacobo didn't like being pushed around. "You are. . . ?" he

called after him boldly.

"Byensii. Kakwa tribe," the boy said proudly. "Same

as President Idi Amin. The Muslims are running the country now. So watch yourself, Christian boy."

Yacobo watched the boy swagger away. Now he understood why his sister, Faisi, said, "I'm not political." He didn't care what tribe someone belonged to. He just wanted to make some new friends and get a good education.

There had been another terrible incident at the university. The warden in charge of the women's residence where the Kenyan girl had lived had been scheduled to give her testimony at court. But the day before the hearing, the warden had been arrested in broad daylight, taken away, and killed. Now Yacobo's parents were *really* worried about Faisi; he didn't want them to worry about him, too, so he didn't tell them about what had happened at his own school.

Besides, they were busy with their new jobs. Theo drove the archbishop on official business, picked up visitors at the international airport in nearby Entebbe, about thirty miles from Kampala, and kept the cars running. Eunika was often called on to cook for the archbishop's many guests. It seemed that every Christian mission worker or evangelist or church official was hosted by the archbishop and his wife at one time or another.

One Sunday in late June, Theo came home from the airport looking flustered and upset. "Have you heard the news?" he asked, turning on the kitchen radio and trying to find a station amid all the static.

Yacobo looked up from his homework that he was doing at the kitchen table.

"Theo, what—?" Eunika began. She was chopping vegetables for that night's supper.

"A group of Arab terrorists hijacked a plane full of Israeli passengers and forced it down at Entebbe airport! I was supposed to pick up one of the archbishop's guests at Entebbe, but they've diverted all planes to other countries." Theo gave up on the fickle radio.

"Why, Taata?" Yacobo asked, using the childhood name for his father.

Theo shrugged. "From what I heard, they're demanding the release of political prisoners." The big man shook his head. "Israel won't do it. They never cooperate with terrorists. But . . . the hijackers said they'd start shooting hostages if they didn't."

"O Lord, have mercy," said Eunika, putting down her chopping knife. "Let's pray for the hostages right now."

The next day, the hijacking was all anyone at school could talk about. Byensii, the Senior 4 student, was talking loudly to a wide-eyed group of boys. "Those hijackers were smart landing at Entebbe," he smirked. "They knew Idi Amin would protect them."

"Why would the president protect a bunch of foreign terrorists?" Yacobo spoke up. Immediately he was sorry he'd said anything.

Byensii turned on him. "What do *you* know, Christian boy?" he sneered. "Because he's a Muslim and all Muslims stick together. And *nobody* stands in Idi Amin's way . . . nobody." He jabbed a finger at Yacobo's chest just as the school bell rang to call them inside.

Three days . . . four days . . . five days went by, and still the hijacked plane sat on the ground at Entebbe airport. The Israelis seemed willing to talk to the terrorists, and so the deadline for shooting hostages was extended. Archbishop Luwum called for national prayer. News on the radio and in the newspapers gave lots of coverage to the terrorists' demands.

But after a few days Yacobo quit caring about it and tried to concentrate on his new classes. He had a full schedule—geography, Ugandan history, English, Swahili, general science, algebra, and advanced writing, as well as soccer. It was tempting to spend extra time on his writing assignments, but he knew he had to keep up in his other subjects if he wanted to stay in this school.

After attending worship at the Namirembe Cathedral on Sunday, July 4, Eunika Kabaza served a light lunch for Archbishop and Mrs. Luwum and several visiting district bishops. When Yacobo's mother came back to the Kabaza apartment, she said, "Yacobo, the archbishop would like you to come see him in his study." She looked at him suspiciously. "You haven't been fooling around and getting into trouble, have you?"

"No, Mama!" he protested.

Why does the archbishop want to see me? Yacobo wondered anxiously, tucking in his shirttail as he hurried into the main part of the house. The house was cool and quiet. At the study door he stopped. He could hear voices inside. Taking a breath for courage, he knocked.

"Come in," said a pleasant voice.

Archbishop Luwum and several other men in clergy collars were sitting in comfortable chairs, leaning slightly toward one another as if they had been having a lively discussion that Yacobo had interrupted.

"Ah, it's Yacobo Kabaza," the archbishop said to the other men. "Sit down, young man."

Yacobo sat, wondering nervously what he was doing here.

"I understand you have a serious interest in writing."

Yacobo nodded. "Yes, sir."

"My fellow bishops and I have been discussing plans for the Centennial," the archbishop explained kindly. Janini Luwum was a short, stocky man, dark skinned like the tribes in the north, with a wide, flat nose. "Of course, each bishop will plan special events for his own district, but many believers plan to come to Kampala for the main celebrations—"

"And we are eager to tell the history of the church in Uganda in a way that will be interesting to young and old alike," interrupted one of the other bishops.

Again Yacobo nodded, feeling puzzled. Why were they telling him these things?

Janini Luwum seemed to sense the boy's bewilderment. "Yacobo, have you heard about the boy martyrs in King Mwanga's court?"

Yacobo found his voice. "Yes, sir, a little." He tried to remember what his father had told them in the car on the way to Kampala about the three servant boys who had been killed for becoming Christians.

"Bishop Wani here has an idea of presenting a play at the Centennial celebrations about these young martyrs who gave their lives for Christ, to be performed by our youth. We have enjoyed much religious freedom in this country up to the present, but dark storm clouds are gathering over Uganda. Tensions are growing, both politically and religiously. Some people are already suffering; many more may suffer in the future. We must encourage one another to have the faith that these young martyrs had."

Yacobo thought he should nod again, but his bewilderment was growing. What did this have to do with him?

"We need someone to write this play," the archbishop said. "Festo Kivengere seems to think highly of your writing potential. Would you be willing to take on this task?"

Yacobo's eyes widened in astonishment. He opened his mouth, but no words came out.

"It would mean doing a lot of research," the archbishop cautioned. "Possibly we could arrange for you to use the university library to find resources. Your writing teacher could supervise your progress. It would be a lot of work. But it would also be a great contribution to our Centennial celebration. What do you think?"

"Oh yes, sir! I mean . . . I would like to try," he heard himself saying. "It would be an honor." No sooner had he opened his mouth than Yacobo felt a rush of fear. Could he write a play? To be performed before thousands of people? What if he failed? What if—

There was a knock on the study door. All eyes turned as an excited Theo Kabaza stuck his head in the door. "Please excuse me for interrupting, Archbishop Luwum," said Theo. His eyes blinked with surprise at seeing Yacobo sitting in the archbishop's study. "We just heard news—last night a band of Israeli commandos landed at Entebbe airport in a surprise attack and freed all the hostages from the hijacked plane! All the terrorists were killed, as well as the Israeli commander."

There was a stunned silence in the room. Bishop Wani murmured, "Praise God the ordeal is over."

Someone else said, "But how did the Israelis get into Uganda? This is going to be very embarrassing for Idi Amin."

Archbishop Luwum interrupted. "One moment, gentlemen. Yacobo, you may go now. Talk to your parents and give me an answer soon."

Yacobo rose and walked to the door, where his father waited. As father and son shut the door behind them, Yacobo heard the archbishop say in a sober voice, "Brothers, I smell trouble."

Chapter 3

Arrested!

YACOBO COULDN'T GET A WORD IN EDGEWISE that night as the family first gathered for tea at six o'clock, then supper at nine. Talk, talk, talk about the Israeli commando raid on Entebbe airport. Apparently the Israeli commandos had flown four Hercules transport planes undetected at low altitude into Entebbe, unloaded a black Mercedes identical to President Amin's personal car, and used an Idi Amin lookalike as a decoy to approach the plane. Taken by surprise, all the terrorists were killed and the hostages loaded quickly into the transport planes. The entire rescue had taken less than an hour.

Blasio was excited by the res- cue. Jumping up from his chair, he held an imaginary machine gun and "blasted away" at imaginary terrorists.

"Stop it, Blasio," said his mother sharply. "Christians cannot be happy when anyone is killed, not even our enemies. The hijackers were bad men; what they did was wrong. But I wish . . . I am sorry they lost their lives. We must pray for their families."

"The trouble is not over," warned Theo. "I heard the bishops say that this raid is very embarrassing for President Amin. To have Israeli commandos use a car like his and a lookalike of himself as a decoy— he is probably furious. There may be trouble."

"What kind of trouble?" asked Blasio eagerly, still making shooting noises with his mouth.

Eunika and Theo Kabaza exchanged a look. "I don't know," Theo said. "But I want you children to stay close to home."

Yacobo groaned. How could he do research on the boy martyrs if he had to stay close to home? The archbishop had even suggested the university library. This would be the perfect excuse to go there!

"Yacobo! Are you asleep?" asked his mother. "I asked what the archbishop wanted to see you about."

Yacobo looked around the table. His father, mother, and brother were all looking at him curiously. He took a deep breath. "Oh. I almost forgot in all the excitement," he said casually. "Archbishop Luwum asked me if I would write a play for the Centennial celebrations next year—about the boy martyrs in King Mwanga's court. You know, the servant boys you were telling us about, Taata."

"A play? For the Centennial?" said his father,

astonished. "But you've never written a play before."

"Well, now," said his mother, beaming, "that doesn't mean he can't. The archbishop must have faith in his ability. But, son, we really don't know much about that story. How will you learn all you need to know to write a whole play?"

"You are right, Mama!" Yacobo saw his opportunity. "The archbishop says I need to do a lot of research—probably at the university library. That way I can find out all I need to know about the Kabaka kings and what happened when the first missionaries came to Uganda and—"

Eunika Kabaza shook her head. "No, no. Not the university library. It is too dangerous. Didn't you hear what your father just said? There could be trouble in the city."

"But, Mama—!"

Theo Kabaza put up his hand. "No more, Yacobo. We will talk about it later."

Yacobo's writing teacher, Mr. Wabaki, readily agreed to supervise the play project. He, too, recommended that Yacobo do research at the university library as part of the learning experience. But Yacobo's parents hesitated. It seemed too dangerous. Idi Amin was blustering again, condemning the Israelis on the radio; the number of soldiers on street corners increased, and so did random searches of cars and homes. Rumors of arrests and missing persons continued to surface. Festo Kivengere arrived back in the country just in time to be ordered, along with the archbishop and many other religious leaders in Kampala, to the conference centre to hear Idi Amin's outraged version of the "raid on Entebbe."

Whether Bishop Kivengere spoke to Yacobo's parents while he was in town, or whether it was just a gradual sense that "life must go on," Yacobo wasn't sure. But in August, Theo and Eunika reluctantly agreed to let him take the matatus from his school to Makerere University twice a week to use the library. But because he was only a high school student, he was not allowed to check out any books; he had to use them at the library.

Yacobo didn't mind. That meant he had to go more often in order to read and take notes for the play project. Sometimes he did his other homework there; it was quiet and peaceful and he didn't have to put up with his annoying little brother.

One afternoon after Yacobo had been coming to the library for a couple of weeks, he was struggling through a big book on the history of the kings of Uganda when he heard a teasing voice at his elbow. "Hey, big boy. At this rate, you're going to graduate from the university before I do."

Yacobo looked up into the grinning face of his sister. "Faisi!" he said. His parents had forbidden him to just wander around the university campus looking for his sister, so he was glad she had found him in the library. Her hair was cut short in the boyish style popular on campus, and her warm brown skin seemed to glow with good health and laughter. Today she wore a white skirt and red blouse with no

jewelry, and her arms cradled a stack of textbooks.

"How's the play going?" she asked, flopping down beside him and dumping her books on the table.

He shrugged. "Haven't started writing the play yet. I'm still trying to get background on the story about the boy martyrs."

"So what have you found out so far?" Faisi asked.

Yacobo looked at his sister in surprise. She actually sounded interested. At home his mother and father mostly seemed relieved when he got home safely from the library, and only as an afterthought asked, "How's the project going?" When he said, "Fine," they'd say, "Good, good."

But Faisi was actually asking. Eagerly Yacobo scanned the notes he'd written down. "It's a lot more interesting than I thought," he said. "A hundred years ago, Uganda was still ruled by the Kabaka kings. In 1896, Uganda became a British protectorate, and then we got independence back in the 1950s—but you know all that stuff."

He scanned his notes. "Oh, here's something interesting. In 1877, two English missionaries—one was named Wilson, the other Shergold-Smith—walked nine hundred miles from the Indian Ocean until they reached Lake Victoria. Then they sailed two hundred miles on Lake Victoria and landed on the northern shore at Entebbe. They were welcomed with a great ceremony by King Kabaka Mutesa, who had become a follower of the Christian faith from talking to Henry Stanley, the English journalist—"

"You mean the newspaper writer who came to

Africa looking for David Livingstone? He was a Christian?" asked Faisi. "I mean, I know that David Livingstone was a great missionary explorer. But I didn't know that Stanley was a Christian or that he converted King Mutesa."

"I guess so," Yacobo said. His eyes were bright with excitement. He had never really liked history before in school, but it was fun finding things out for himself and piecing bits of things together to discover a story. "Anyway, Mutesa wanted to learn more about the Christian religion from the missionaries," Yacobo grinned slyly, "and he was also hoping he would learn how to make guns and gunpowder from these Englishmen."

Now it was Faisi's turn to roll her eyes. "Oh, thank you very much. Uganda is in great shape today because we have guns and gunpowder." A bitter edge crept into her voice.

"Anyway," continued Yacobo, "that meeting of King Mutesa and the English missionaries is considered the beginning of the Christian church in Uganda. That's why we're celebrating the Centennial next year in '77."

"But . . . if King Mutesa was a Christian, why did he kill his servant boys for becoming Christians?" Faisi asked.

"Wrong king," Yacobo smirked. "King Mutesa died, and his son, Kabaka Mwanga, became king. Mwanga followed the Muslim faith, and when his father died, he decided he would squash this new religion. So when he discovered that three of his own servant boys were Christians, he decided to torture and kill them as a lesson to anyone else who was thinking about becoming a Christian."

"Gruesome. How old were they?"

"I'm not sure about the middle one. But the oldest was fifteen, and the youngest was only eleven."

"Fifteen and eleven!" Faisi said, looking a little sick. "That's just a year older than you and Blasio."

Yacobo stared at her. He hadn't thought of it like that. Suddenly the story he was writing about felt a lot more real.

"I have to go," Faisi said suddenly, collecting her books. "There's a student meeting about recent government actions and I—what? What's the matter?"

Yacobo stared at his sister. "But you told our parents that you aren't political," he said accusingly. "They worry about you all the time."

Faisi looked uncomfortable. "Well, I'm really *not* political. But Charity Kivengere says we Christian students can't close our eyes to what's happening in our country." She leaned closer to Yacobo and lowered her voice. "It's getting really bad, Yacobo. Idi Amin is wrecking Uganda, and nobody's stopping him! His soldiers arrest people who disagree with him, but they never get a trial; they just disappear. Hundreds of Asian business people have been kicked out of the country, and their businesses have been given to people who don't know how to run them. It's crazy! Idi Amin acts like Uganda is just a bunch of warring tribes instead of a modern democratic country. He's putting our progress back a hundred years!"

Yacobo stared openmouthed at his sister. He'd never heard her talk like this.

"Anyway, I've got to go," Faisi said. "And maybe you should go home, too, Yacobo. But . . . don't say anything to Mama and Taata, all right?"

Yacobo watched his sister walk out of the library, then he turned back to his book. He hadn't gotten a chance to finish telling Faisi what he'd learned about the boy martyrs. There was more—a lot more. *Well, he thought, she can go to her dumb old meeting.* He'd go home when he was good and ready.

Yacobo finally put the book back on the shelf and gathered up his own schoolbooks. His stomach growled, and for the first time he realized he had stayed later than usual and had better hurry if he was going to be on time for tea. He noticed that no one else seemed to be in the library.

Hurrying out of the library, Yacobo headed across campus for the front gate of the university, where he could catch a matatu. But before he reached the gate, he heard a loud noise and the squeal of tires. Suddenly several army trucks roared through the front gate and sped past him. Yacobo stared after them. What were army trucks doing on the university campus? And why were they in such a hurry? With a sick feeling, he realized the trucks were heading in the direction of the residence halls where the students lived!

Without thinking, Yacobo ran after the trucks.

By the time he caught up with them, soldiers were running into the residence halls and dragging students out. Screams and shouts filled the air.

Badly frightened, Yacobo ducked behind the corner of a building out of sight. Peering around the corner, he saw many students trying to run away, but the soldiers hit them with the butts of their guns and made them crawl over the rough gravel toward the trucks. Cries and screams mingled with the harsh shouts of the soldiers.

The soldiers were rounding up both young men and young women and making them climb in the back of the open trucks. How many? One hundred? Two? Suddenly he saw a girl wearing a red blouse being pushed and shoved onto a truck. Right behind her was another girl in a blue blouse, a few years older, who looked familiar.

It was Faisi! And Charity Kivengere!

In horror, Yacobo watched as the rear gates of the trucks were slammed shut, each one full of frightened students packed together like livestock. Yacobo kept his eyes on the red and blue blouses as the idling engines were gunned and the trucks spun out toward the front gate of the university and were gone.

Stunned, Yacobo didn't know what to do. People were running this way and that, shouting to one another and crying. Where were they taking his sister and Charity? What was going to happen to them?

A cold knot of fear in Yacobo's chest made it difficult to breathe. He had to get home. He had to tell his mother and father!

Chapter 4

Law and Disorder

"Oh, Lord, not Faisi!" cried Eunika Kabaza, crumpling to a heap on the ground when she heard that her daughter had been arrested.

Yacobo could hardly remember how he got home. Somehow word had already reached the archbishop's residence that a large number of students at the university had been arrested, and when Yacobo stumbled into the courtyard, he was greeted with cries of relief. But as he gasped out his story of soldiers dragging students out of their residences and hauling them away by the truckloads—including his sister and Charity Kivengere—relief turned to shock and alarm.

"Theo, let my wife stay with

Eunika," said Archbishop Luwum, taking charge of the situation. "Will you drive me to the university? I must find out for myself what has happened. We must send an advocate to the prison to speak on behalf of the students who have been arrested. And the students and professors whose friends and classmates were taken away need pastoral care. Oh—" he turned to his assistant—"get word right away to Festo and Mera Kivengere about Charity."

Yacobo watched his father drive off with the archbishop and several others from his pastoral staff. Going back to his family's apartment, he saw that his mother had stopped her tears and was down on her knees, her Bible open on a chair before her. She and Mary Luwum read Scripture, prayed, and cried together. Then Eunika got up, fed the boys their supper, helped Blasio with his homework, and put him to bed. Even after Yacobo went to bed, he could hear her reading the Bible and praying far into the night.

When Yacobo woke up the next morning, he had a terrible feeling inside, like someone had died, but at first he couldn't remember who or why. Then he remembered: Faisi had been arrested yesterday and taken to Idi Amin's prison. Icy fingers of fear gripped his heart. He had never heard of anyone actually leaving that prison alive.

Yacobo pulled on the clothes he'd worn the day before. There was no way he could go to school today, not with his sister in danger. He was prepared to fight his mother on this point, but she said nothing about school as he came into the tiny kitchen of their apartment. Eunika's eyes were puffy and her face strained, as if she had not slept all night.

"Sit down and have some breakfast, Yacobo," she said, putting a bowl of cornmeal on the table, along with some goat's milk and honey.

"Not hungry," he mumbled.

Eunika stopped what she was doing, took Yacobo by the shoulders, and looked into his eyes. "Whatever happens, Yacobo," she said gently, "we must remember that there is nothing—nothing!—that can happen that will separate our Faisi from the love of God."

Yacobo looked away, a lump tight in his throat. He knew those verses—Romans 8:38 and 39. They were easy verses to say when he was learning them in Bible class, but it wasn't easy now that his sister was in Idi Amin's death prison.

All that morning they waited. And then when they thought they couldn't stand not knowing what was happening one more minute, the archbishop's car turned in at the gate and pulled up in front of the house.

"Mama, Mama!" yelled Blasio, dancing up and down. "Taata's back!"

Eunika Kabaza, Yacobo, Mary Luwum, and others who had gathered to wait with them came running. Car doors opened. And then Blasio screamed, "They've got Faisi!"

Yacobo could hardly believe his eyes, but it was true! Theo got out of the driver's seat, then helped his daughter out of the backseat. Eunika and the boys rushed toward her, then stopped.

Faisi's face was bruised, one eye was swollen, and cuts were all over her head and shoulders.

"Oh, Faisi," wailed Eunika and burst into tears.

"I'm all right, Mama—really I am," said Faisi softly. A strange smile was on her face. "Let's go inside, and I will tell you all about it."

"No, first we must attend to those cuts," Theo said firmly, putting a protective arm around his daughter and guiding her inside.

When Faisi's cuts had been cleaned and the worst ones bandaged, Mrs. Luwum brought tea for everyone, and they all gathered in the Kabazas' small sitting room to hear Faisi's story.

"We were all terribly frightened," she said, her voice soft. Yacobo had to strain to hear. "The soldiers kept hitting us and pushing us around. One student asked, 'Why are we being arrested? What did we do?' And the soldier in charge—a captain, I think—spit and said something about the students at the university going on strike and plotting to overthrow the government."

"What?" said her mother, shocked.

"It's not true, Mama," said Faisi. "I mean, it *is* true that many of the students got very upset when the lady warden—who is . . . who was . . . very popular with students—was arrested and killed just because she was going to testify on behalf of that Kenyan girl! We were so upset that sometimes we didn't go to our classes, and instead we met together in small groups to talk and support one another. But we weren't causing a disruption, and we certainly weren't plotting to overthrow the government!" Faisi's eyes flashed.

"That's all right, sugar," said Theo. "Go on and tell your mother what happened at the prison."

Faisi took a breath. "They made us line up and . . . and the soldier at the gate was beating the students with a spiked club as they entered. There were over two hundred of us, and they crowded us into a locked room. All of us were frightened, some were crying. And many were hurt or bleeding in some way. We gave each other first aid as best we could."

Faisi looked at the archbishop. "Charity was wonderful—Festo and Mera Kivengere would have been proud of her. Many of the students were Christians, and Charity gathered us together and we all started praying quietly. We knew we were in serious danger, but as we prayed, the terror left us, and we began to feel calm and unafraid. Someone said Jesus would want us to forgive our enemies. So we prayed that God would forgive the soldiers who had hurt us, because they didn't know what they were doing!"

The light returned to Faisi's face. "And then another student reminded us that nothing in this world can separate us from the love of God—not even death. And if we died, we would go to heaven to be with Jesus, our Savior. And suddenly our spirits felt . . . lighter, and we even began to laugh with relief and joy."

Yacobo looked with astonishment from his sister to his mother. That was the same verse his mother had quoted that morning!

"But how did you get out, Faisi?" asked Blasio, crowding close to his big sister. "Did you escape?" His eyes glowed with high hopes for a jail-break story.

"We got out by . . . prayer." She looked around the room. "I know you all were praying. There's no other way to explain it. The military chief-of-staff came into the room where we were being kept, and he seemed surprised to see us sitting so peacefully. We greeted him respectfully, and he even ordered tea for all of us! He gave us a long lecture on patriotism and being good citizens, then he ordered us to go back to the university and attend our classes and not cause any trouble! The same trucks that brought us to the prison took us back . . . and there was Taata and Archbishop Luwum and the Catholic cardinal holding prayer meetings on campus for us!"

"Glory!" cried Eunika and spontaneously burst into a song of praise. The others joined in, even Yacobo and Blasio. But even as they sang, Yacobo had a feeling of unreality. Had this really happened to his own sister? They'd been so terrified they'd never see her again, and now here she was telling this incredible story. As the singing and thanksgiving continued, Yacobo slipped into the bedroom he shared with Blasio, took out a sheet of school paper, and began to write down the story Faisi had told.

Faisi insisted on going back to school after a few days of recovery with her family, but there were no more trips to the university library for Yacobo. Idi Amin's soldiers now seemed completely out of control. There was another attack on the university—

this time on just the men's residence hall. No students were arrested but many were badly beaten and injured. "President Amin is afraid of a coup," said Theo grimly. "He's trying to make the students too frightened to organize any protests."

Both soldiers and ordinary criminals felt free to loot stores and homes and beat up on citizens. Law and order was breaking down everywhere. Even though the Kabazas and other families tried to go about their daily tasks, Theo drove Yacobo and Blasio to and from school each day in his old taxi, just to be safe.

Yacobo was frustrated. He still needed more information before he could begin writing the Centennial play. His writing teacher refused to supply the information he needed. "Knowing how to get information is a critical tool if you want to be a writer, Yacobo," Mr. Wabaki said. "You will find a way. In the meantime, you can organize the material you do have and begin writing a rough outline of your story, scene by scene."

Yacobo didn't want to do it that way. How would he know where to begin his story if he didn't have all the facts yet? Would he begin with the Kabaka kings? Or with the English missionaries? Or maybe with the boys themselves.

Trouble at school was another problem. The high school headmaster and teachers kept strict order, but whenever they were out of sight, Byensii, the Senior 4 Kakwa boy, and a gang of other Kakwa students lost no time bullying Yacobo and other students they disliked. Every time Yacobo was tempted to tell his parents about it, he clamped his mouth shut. He knew they wouldn't need much of an excuse to pull him from the school, writing class or no writing class.

And then, in November, Yacobo found a way to continue his writing.

According to Archbishop Luwum, there was a new openness to spiritual things on the campus of Makerere University ever since the arrests and beatings of students last August. He asked Festo Kivengere to come to Kampala and lead a "mission" on campus for the university students. It would be a joint mission along with an evangelistic Catholic bishop, lasting a week.

Faisi Kabaza and Charity Kivengere were excited about the mission. They'd been witnessing to the other young women in their dorm, who had come to respect these Christians who'd been arrested and beaten but didn't react with hatred or anger.

Yacobo had his own reason for being glad to see Festo Kivengere. As he lay in bed at night he hatched his plan: Bishop Kivengere would be staying at the Anglican guest house during the mission and going to the university each day. If Yacobo chose the right moment to ask, surely his parents would allow him to ride along with their very own bishop and use the university library during the preaching services. No soldiers would dare attack the university while both the Protestants and the Catholics were holding evangelistic services on campus.

The plan worked. Yacobo asked his parents when Festo Kivengere stopped in briefly to visit them, and the bishop immediately said, "Why, I'd be more than happy to take Yacobo with me to the university and return him safely to you. Anything to help this play project along—it's a wonderful opportunity for him." What could Theo and Eunika say?

In the library on the first night of the mission, Yacobo read some more about the Kabaka kings and what happened when King Mwanga had the three servant boys killed by fire. People had been weeping and their parents were pleading with them to give up their Christian faith. But they would not. They even sent a message to the king: "Tell His Majesty that he has put our bodies in the fire, but we won't be long in the fire. Soon we shall be with Jesus, which is much better. But ask him to repent . . . or he will land in a place of eternal fire."

Then the boys sang a song that later became known as the "Martyrs' Song" in all the Christian churches in Uganda. Yacobo remembered hearing the song, though he hadn't known the story behind it. He sang to himself the little bit that he could remember: "'O that I had wings like the angels. I would fly away and be with Jesus!'"

Yacobo kept reading. King Mwanga became angry because he couldn't frighten the boys into denying their faith. He ordered his warriors to chop off their arms and then throw them alive into the fire. The youngest boy, named Yusufu, pleaded, "Please don't cut off my arms. I will not struggle in the fire that takes me to Jesus!"

The people watching were shaken by such heroic strength in such young boys. What kind of faith was this that could not be controlled by torture and death? That very day, forty adults put their faith in Jesus.

Yacobo slowly closed the book. Did he have that kind of faith in Jesus? Oh yes, he believed in Jesus and wanted to be a good Christian. But . . . would he not be afraid? Would he cling to his faith if he were faced with torture and death?

A hard little seed of doubt, like a cherry pit stuck in his throat, began to worry him. If he couldn't imagine having that kind of faith, how could he write about it in a believable way?

Walking slowly, Yacobo left the library and went over to the building where the two bishops—one Anglican, one Catholic—were holding their mission. Festo Kivengere was standing in front of a group of students who were listening attentively. He was not preaching to them, just talking.

". . . knew I could no longer keep on hating my stepfather with Christ in my heart," the bishop was saying. "But the only way to quit hating my stepfather was to forgive him. I didn't want to do that! He had mistreated my mother! But the Bible tells us to 'walk in the light,' and that meant I had to confess my hatred and forgive him. My knees were shaking as I walked up the path to my stepfather's house. He was surprised to see me, and when he heard why I had come, he was very quiet. Then he put his arms around me. As he did so, I realized the hatred was gone. I was able to love him with God's love."

The students were very quiet.

"But if you think that was hard," Festo Kivengere joked, "it was easy compared to the time I had to forgive a white man!" The students laughed.

Bishop Kivengere went on to tell a story about how he had held resentment for many years against an English missionary who had acted superior toward him. The white man did not treat the Ugandans as equals. Instead, he made Festo feel like a child, even though he was a grown man. "But when I went to him and asked him to forgive me for my resentment toward him, it was as if a wall came down between us." The bishop looked around at the students. "Many times since then I have proved that the Cross of Jesus is the end of racial prejudice and separating walls of all kinds."

Yacobo thought about what Bishop Kivengere was saying. He knew the Bible said a person should ask for forgiveness if he does something wrong to someone—but weren't the stepfather and the white missionary in the bishop's story the ones who were wrong? Why did Festo ask their forgiveness?

As if reading his mind, Bishop Kivengere said to the students, "I could forgive them because Christ died for me and forgave me *even while I was still a sinner*. And even though their actions were wrong, so was my hatred and resentment."

A young man put his hand in the air. "This 'walking in the light'—I don't understand what it means."

The bishop smiled his winning smile. "Jesus said,

'I am the light of the world.' When we let His light into our lives, His Word shines on things that are not like Jesus so they can be cleansed. And His light shines on our brother or sister, making them precious." He paused and grinned. "I said precious, not perfect." Laughter again rippled around the room.

Then he was serious again. "Some of you have heard the story of the students who were arrested and beaten last August. My daughter Charity was among them. She tells me that the Christian students prayed for the soldiers who abused them and forgave them. How is that possible? Because those students knew that their own salvation is only possible because of Christ's love, grace, and forgiveness—when He covered their sins with His own blood on the cross. If God can love and forgive us like that, can we do any less toward our fellow sinners?"

It was quite late when the bishop was finally free to leave. Students were still praying in small groups. All the way home in Bishop Kivengere's car, Yacobo was quiet. His thoughts skittered around uncomfortably, like drops of water on a hot skillet. The boy Yusufu, only eleven years old, had been willing to die by fire rather than give up his faith. . . . Festo Kivengere asked his mean stepfather to forgive him for his hatred. . . . Faisi and Charity forgave the soldiers who hurt them. . . .

He felt a growing uneasiness about agreeing to write the play. It was beginning to feel too close and personal.

Chapter 5

King Herod

THE MISSION AT THE UNIVERSITY was over. "God did a mighty work among the students!" Festo Kivengere reported to the archbishop and others who had gathered around to see him off. His trim moustache only accented the wide grin on his face. "The tragic events of this year created an eagerness to hear about spiritual things. Lukewarm Christians have received a new fire to live their faith. Other students put their trust in Christ for the first time. It was a great day for the Gospel! And," he winked at Yacobo, who was hanging around the edge of the send-off, "I think many of the students were astonished when the

Catholic bishop gave me a big hug in front of everyone and said, 'I love you, Festo!' Right, Yacobo?"

Yacobo grinned, too. He'd been amazed himself.

"Festo, are you sure you can't stay for the meeting with the cardinal and the grand mufti?" said Archbishop Luwum, shaking the bishop's hand in a reluctant good-bye. "It could be very important."

Festo shook his head. "I must get back to my district. I have been gone too long this year. But I will notify all the churches in the Kigezi district. We will be praying for you."

Bishop Kivengere said good-byes all around. When he came to Blasio, he punched the youngster playfully on the shoulder and said, "I hear you volunteered to be King Herod in the Christmas pageant at the cathedral. Is that so?"

Blasio giggled. "Yes! He's the big bad king who kills all the babies trying to get rid of Jesus." He made his face look fierce.

"Hush, Blasio!" scolded Eunika Kabaza. "You don't have to be so gruesome."

"But he was really bad, Mama!" Blasio protested.

"He was definitely a wicked king," Bishop Kivengere agreed. "Well, Blasio, I know you'll do a good job. You have, shall we say, a natural acting talent."

The adults laughed. Blasio's antics were becoming well known around the archbishop's household.

Yacobo rolled his eyes. He felt a little jealous hearing Festo Kivengere praise Blasio's "talent." *He* was the one who had the talent. Hadn't the bishop said so himself? *"Great potential to be a writer,"* he'd said. In fact, Yacobo couldn't imagine Blasio doing a serious job in a play. His brother was just a clown.

As Bishop Kivengere's car turned out of the gate and disappeared into traffic for the long ride back to Kabale, the rest of the household went back inside. Yacobo tugged at his father's sleeve. "Taata, what did the archbishop mean when he talked about the cardinal and the crand mufti? What is a grand mufti, anyway?"

Theo Kabaza scratched his chin thoughtfully. "He's the head of the Muslim religion here in Uganda. If the Catholic cardinal, the Protestant archbishop, and the Grand Mufti are planning a meeting, why, that represents nearly the whole of Uganda. I wonder . . ." Theo did not finish his sentence. But Yacobo thought his father looked a little worried.

School was out the month of December for the "winter holiday." Faisi came home from the university to spend the holidays with her family. Soon Christmas celebrations were in full swing. Advent services each Sunday at the cathedral—celebrating the "advent" or "coming near" of the Christ—were full of joyful worship. Christmastime had always been special back home in Kabale, but there was a special excitement here at the big cathedral in Kampala. Colorful banners were added and new candles lit each week in anticipation of Christ's birth. But the really big celebration, they'd heard, would be

Christmas Eve, when the children and young people would put on their Christmas pageant and the archbishop would deliver his annual Christmas sermon, which was broadcast on radio to the whole country.

Before school let out, Yacobo's writing teacher had suggested that he use the winter holiday to begin writing the first draft of the Centennial play. But where was he going to find a quiet place to write? Faisi was now using the family sitting room as her bedroom. Blasio was always running in and out of the boys' sleeping room or practicing his King Herod lines in a loud, pompous voice. Finally Yacobo took his problem to the archbishop.

Janini Luwum was more than gracious. "Let's see . . . you may use my study, Yacobo. In fact, tomorrow I will be at a meeting all day. No one will disturb you. You should get a lot of writing done, eh?"

The next morning Theo Kabaza brought the archbishop's official car to the front door. Several other district bishops—Yacobo recognized Silvanus Wani—who had come to Kampala for this meeting got into the car with the archbishop. Before he got back into the driver's seat, Theo Kabaza mouthed the words "grand mufti" to his son, who was watching from the front steps. "Pray."

Yacobo gave a slight nod. So this was the big meeting with the Catholic cardinal and the grand mufti. He went back inside the house and, feeling a little out of place, headed for the archbishop's study. He wondered what they were going to talk about. Maybe they were going to argue religion. But . . . it was one thing to talk about cooperation and brotherhood between Protestants and Catholics. After all, Catholics were Christians, too. But the Muslims—why, they didn't even believe Jesus was God's Son!

But Yacobo soon forgot about the archbishop's meeting as he concentrated on his story. He would do as his teacher had suggested and write a summary of the whole story, scene by scene. Once that was done, he would go back and work each scene into a script for a play, using dialogue to tell the story.

"I'll probably have to have a narrator between scenes," he mused to himself, spreading out his notes on the table the archbishop had said he could use. "But . . . maybe not." He felt a little thrill of excitement. He had never tried using just dialogue, the things people say, to tell a story. But that was the way a play was written. Just using dialogue. Nothing else.

Yacobo worked all morning, and he was surprised when his mother brought him some plantains, bread, and tea with milk and sugar for his noon meal. All afternoon he kept working, telling the story of King Kabaka Mutesa gladly greeting the English missionaries in 1877 in one scene. The next scene was the death of King Mutesa and the new king's vow to purge Christianity from Uganda. Scene by scene, Yacobo summarized the story, reviewing his notes from time to time to make sure he was getting everything in. After he had made martyrs out of his three servant boys, King Mwanga sent his warriors from village to village to kill any Christians they found. But for every Christian they killed, it seemed ten more declared they wanted to become Christians. Yacobo chuckled to himself. That would be a good scene. Christians popping up all over the place.

Voices outside the archbishop's study made Yacobo realize he'd lost all track of time. He heard the archbishop saying, "Yes, yes, Mary, it was a good meeting. We agreed on many resolutions protesting what is happening in the government. . . . Specifically? Why, the president's intelligence officers have been given power to arrest and execute people with no trial! Soldiers and common criminals alike are looting and killing . . . ordinary citizens are being harassed and searched in their own homes." The door opened and the voices continued. "We've sent a message to the president, asking for a personal meeting with him to present these—oh, Yacobo!" The archbishop, with Mrs. Luwum at his side, stopped in surprise at seeing Yacobo in the room. "I forgot you were using my study today. Did you get a lot of writing done?"

"Oh yes, sir," said Yacobo, quickly standing up and gathering his pages together.

"No, no, just leave them," said the archbishop. "I have no visitors scheduled tomorrow, do I, dear? I may do some reading and sermon preparation. We can work quietly together, eh?" He smiled warmly at Yacobo.

The next day, Yacobo felt strange doing his writing in the same room with the archbishop. He wished he could work alone, but it was the archbishop's study, after all. Soon, however, he forgot the man on the other side of the room and began to fill out some of the scenes he'd sketched the day before.

The telephone rang. The archbishop answered and Yacobo wondered if he should leave the room. "Yes, I'll hold," said the archbishop. He didn't say anything to Yacobo, so the boy shrugged and went back to his writing. Then he heard, "Good morning, Mr. President."

Yacobo was startled. President Idi Amin?

"Yes," said the archbishop, "the cardinal and the grand mufti and I did make a request to meet with you personally." Long pause. "Why did we have a meeting without your permission? I'm sorry, Mr. President, but we have never needed per— . . . Of course. We would gladly have asked for permission if we had known. . . . I see. Yes, of course you may have a copy of the minutes of our meeting. In fact, that's why we requested a meeting with you, to tell you personally about our meeting and— . . . All right. We will send the document to you by personal carrier today. . . . Yes, Mr. President. Good-bye."

Yacobo sat frozen at the table in the archbishop's study. The archbishop seemed to have forgotten that the boy was in the room. He just sat at his desk, his hand still resting on the telephone receiver, frowning in thought. After what seemed like a long time to Yacobo, who scarcely dared to breathe, the archbishop abruptly got up and left the room.

Quickly Yacobo gathered up his papers and left the

study. He didn't feel like writing anymore. He didn't understand what was going on, but he knew one thing: The archbishop was worried about something.

A few days later, fifty delegates from the Church of Uganda—including Archbishop Luwum and Festo Kivengere—boarded a bus bound for Nairobi, Kenya, for the Pan African Christian Leadership Assembly, or PACLA, as it was called. Christian leaders from many African countries met together to encourage and support one another. Billy Graham, the American evangelist, was going to be there, and Festo Kivengere was going to translate for him. The next night, Festo—Uganda's own evangelist—was going to preach.

Yacobo overheard his father tell his mother that he was surprised Idi Amin had given permission for the delegates to leave the country. "That man is so unpredictable," Theo had muttered, shaking his head. "Furious with religious leaders one day, agreeable the next."

Before he left, the archbishop gave Yacobo permission to use his study while he was gone as a quiet place to work on the Centennial play. All week long Yacobo worked on it. But it was slow going. He had come across some new information he wanted to work into the plot. There was another martyr the same year the boy martyrs were killed—Bishop Hannington. Hannington had been sent by the

Church of England to be bishop of East and Central Africa, and his caravan entered Uganda from the east.

But there was an old Ugandan tradition that said, "Beware the stranger who enters the country from the direction of the rising sun. He is dangerous and plans to take over the country!" King Mwanga, not knowing Hannington's purpose, sent warriors to murder the "stranger" before he crossed the Nile River. As the warriors speared him, the dying bishop had said, "I am now going to die at your hands, but I want you to tell your king that my blood has bought this way into the country."

Yacobo had been excited when he discovered this part of the story. The book he read had said the bishop's words came true, because the main roads and railways into Uganda today come from the east.

But telling a story using only dialogue was a lot harder than Yacobo thought it was going to be. Sometimes in a fit of frustration he threw out what he'd written and started over again. And sometimes he just felt stuck.

"Why don't you put it aside for a few days," his sister, Faisi, suggested when he complained to her. "Sometimes when I get stuck writing a paper for one of my classes, if I give it a rest my mind often comes up with fresh ideas when I'm ready to work on it again. Besides, I think Mama can use some extra help. The archbishop has a lot of guests coming into town for the Christmas Eve celebration tonight, and I'm trying to finish Blasio's King Herod costume."

Yacobo was only too glad to put his writing aside.

It was almost a relief to run errands for his mother and help serve some of the meals for the archbishop's guests. He helped his father wash the old taxi and the archbishop's official car. Before he knew it, it was Christmas Eve.

Theo drove Blasio to the cathedral early to get ready for the pageant; then he came back and picked up the archbishop and Mrs. Luwum and the rest of his family. The cathedral was packed not only with people who lived in Kampala but with people who lived in the outlying towns. Beautiful Christmas music swelled from the organ. The choir sang some traditional Ugandan hymns. Then it was time for the pageant.

Yacobo poked Faisi. "I hope Blasio doesn't goof up his lines or make faces trying to make people laugh," he whispered. Faisi rolled her eyes in agreement.

It turned out to be a wonderful pageant. The power of the Christmas story held everyone in awe, even though there were the usual childish flubs as an angel's "halo" fell off and Mary the Mother of Jesus tripped over her robe. But even Yacobo had to grudgingly admit that his brother did a powerful performance as King Herod. The ten-year-old acted with mock delight when the wise men told him about the star, his voice dripping with honey when he said he wanted to worship the new king, too. Then his voice changed to cold cunning as he hatched his evil plot to destroy the baby king.

Then Archbishop Luwum preached his annual Christmas sermon. His theme was the birth of the

Prince of Peace and the factors in their homes and in their nation that destroy peace. He warned the people not to give in to the tribal jealousies that were tearing the government apart. He pled with the people to speak out against violence and bloodshed, but to do it in the love of Christ. Finally, he called on all Christians and people in government to obey the "laws of God."

Yacobo felt uneasy. He remembered that the

archbishop's message was being broadcast on the radio. What if Idi Amin was listening? Would it make him mad?

When the Kabaza family came outside after the Christmas Eve service into the sweet, warm evening, they noticed more than the usual number of soldiers standing on the street corners and army trucks cruising slowly past the cathedral. Instead of waiting to greet people as they normally did, Theo herded his family into the car and took them home, then went back to wait for the archbishop.

While they were waiting for their father to return home, Yacobo idly fiddled with the dial of the radio in the kitchen. Suddenly it crackled to life with the angry voice of Idi Amin.

" . . . some bishops do not support their government," the radio sputtered, "but are preaching rebellion over these very airwaves! Do not listen to their treason! This government deals harshly with anyone who speaks treason!"

Eunika, Faisi, and Yacobo looked at one another in dismay. Blasio, letting off steam by turning somersaults on Faisi's bedroll in the sitting area, was blissfully unaware of the president's speech. No one spoke, but the question was in all their eyes: Was the president publicly threatening the archbishop?

As Yacobo turned off the radio, he heard Faisi mutter, "Uganda's got its own King Herod."

For Christmas, Archbishop Luwum and his wife gave small gifts to their household staff. For the Kabazas, this meant a bonus for Theo and Eunika, a book for Faisi, and American baseball caps for Yacobo and Blasio. The children knelt in traditional Ugandan fashion to express their thanks to the archbishop.

"This boy is to be congratulated," said the archbishop jovially, pumping Blasio's hand as the children got to their feet again. "Young man, you make a *mean* King Herod!"

Everyone laughed.

"You know, Yacobo," said the archbishop, turning to the older boy, "Blasio's performance set me to thinking. Wasn't one of the boy martyrs about Blasio's age?"

Yacobo hesitated. What was the archbishop driving at? "Yes," he admitted. "Yusufu, the youngest, was eleven years old."

The archbishop beamed. "I'm thinking maybe we have found one of our actors for the Centennial play." He patted Blasio on the shoulder. "That would make this play a real family affair!"

All around him, Yacobo's mother, father, and sister nodded and smiled and agreed that it would be a wonderful thing. But Yacobo felt a rush of anger and protest. He didn't want Blasio to play Yusufu! He turned away. Why not? Was he jealous of all the attention Blasio was getting? Yes, a little, he admitted to himself, but it wasn't really that. He couldn't put a finger on it. But it was . . . something else.

Chapter 6

Knock in the Night

NEW YEAR'S DAY, 1977, came and went, and it was time for Faisi and the boys to go back to school. Yacobo was now starting his Senior 2 year. But as he looked at his new class schedule, Yacobo realized his mistake in not finishing the first draft of the Centennial play during the December holiday. He would now have to write the play on top of all his other schoolwork! But, he thought, at least his old enemy, the Kakwa boy, wouldn't be around this term.

But to his dismay, Byensii was leaning against the wall of the school, surrounded by a small gang of admirers, the same old smirk on his face. Yacobo groaned inside. But he shouldn't be surprised, he thought. Many students were kept back until they met the strict educational standards.

"Hey, Christian boy," sneered Byensii, "if you're smart, maybe it's time to change your religion."

A warning flag went up in Yacobo's mind. "What do you mean?"

"Don't you listen to the news? The president is kicking out the Christians in his government and replacing them with good Muslims. Pretty soon Uganda will be a Muslim country . . . and then we're going to walk on you." He laughed.

Yacobo walked into the school without answering. He hated that boy! . . . No, he shouldn't even let that thought into his head. He knew what Bishop Kivengere would say: "You shouldn't judge a whole group of people by the actions of a few." After all, hadn't the grand mufti, the leader of the Muslims, cooperated with the archbishop and the Catholic cardinal in denouncing the violence? And two years ago in Kabale, hadn't the Muslim governor—hostile at first, until Bishop Kivengere reached out to him in friendship—ended up providing government trucks to bring food for the people who attended the forty-year anniversary of the East African Revival?

Still, Yacobo decided to avoid Byensii as much as possible.

Yacobo stayed after school to show his writing teacher the work he'd done on the Centennial play so far. Mr. Wabaki seemed pleased with the scene summaries but challenged Yacobo to finish the first draft of the actual script. "You've got a good grasp of the story," he said, "and a good start on the dialogue in the first scene. But when you finish the first draft, then we can work on the pacing and dramatic tension."

That night after Blasio had fallen asleep, Yacobo sat on his bed and got out his writing tablet. He was working on the second scene, where King Mwanga ties up the three boy servants and threatens to throw them in the fire if they don't give up their faith. But the image of his sister and Charity Kivengere being thrown in the army trucks by the soldiers kept pushing into Yacobo's mind. He shook his head, trying to get rid of the memory. But as he wrote down the brave words spoken by little Yusufu, the youngest of the martyrs, Yacobo suddenly looked over at his little brother, sprawled peacefully in his sleep. In his mind he could almost hear the words spoken in his brother's dramatic voice: *"Please don't cut off my arms!"*

Yacobo threw down his pencil. No! He didn't want Blasio to play the part of Yusufu. How could he write a part for a boy *just like his little brother*? It made the story feel too frightening, too real.

Yacobo let the comings and goings of the archbishop's household that January of 1977 swirl around him without really noticing. He had enough on his mind with homework, working on the play, and trying to avoid Byensii at school.

His father was gone for several days, driving Archbishop Luwum to two different conventions in northern and western Uganda. When they returned, his father reported that the archbishop was really excited about what God had done at these conventions. In northern Gulu, the churches had suffered twenty years of tribal tension and unrest, but at the convention the Holy Spirit had begun healing and reconciliation. In the west, in the shadow of the Ruwenzori Mountains, right in the middle of the archbishop's sermons, people began to sing and weep and come forward to accept Christ! "No one was more amazed than the archbishop himself," said Yacobo's father. "It was truly a work of the Holy Spirit!"

Yacobo also got to see Festo and Mera Kivengere when they came to Kampala and stayed in the Namirembe Guest House after the Kivengeres and Luwums had consecrated a new bishop the last weekend in January. "What an occasion!" Festo exclaimed, beaming, as he sat at the festive table prepared by Eunika Kabaza for the archbishop and his guests. "Sitting in the front were rows of military men, policemen, government officials, clergymen, bishops, Catholic dignitaries, my friend the Muslim governor, and even some of Idi Amin's intelligence officers!"

"You preached a very brave sermon," said Archbishop Luwum somewhat gravely.

"From Acts 20 . . . yes, Paul's charge to church leaders to shepherd their flocks in perilous times," Festo chuckled.

"You didn't stop with a charge to church leaders," Mera Kivengere chided her husband gently. "You talked about government officials who abuse their authority, and challenged those present to use their authority to heal, not hurt."

"But what could I do?" her husband teased. "That was the text for the day on the church calendar!"

Later, Yacobo heard his father and mother talking quietly in the Kabaza kitchen. "I had a strange feeling listening to the sermons preached by Archbishop Luwum and Bishop Kivengere," Theo said in a low voice. "It was almost like . . . like they were saying good-bye."

"Hush, now, don't talk like that," scolded Yacobo's mother. "But we must remember to pray for our spiritual leaders every day. These are difficult times."

The next day when Yacobo arrived home after school, no one was in the apartment. He peeked in the pot simmering on the electric stove and sniffed the delicious smell of goat's meat and vegetables. Grabbing a piece of melon from the refrigerator, he went wandering into the main part of the archbishop's house looking for one of his parents.

As he neared the first-floor entryway, he heard Festo Kivengere's voice, excited and talking faster than usual.

". . . I didn't recognize the man," he was saying. "Mera and I just heard the gunshots out in the street—in broad daylight! When we looked out the window, children were screaming and women were running every which way. Then the men who were shooting went into a building and dragged out this man, tied him up, and took him away."

Yacobo saw his father and Archbishop Luwum standing in the entryway with Bishop Kivengere.

What was going on?

"They weren't ordinary soldiers, you say?" said the archbishop.

"No, the gunmen were dressed in street clothes—colorful shirts, sunglasses—the 'uniform' of the so-called 'Research Unit' or intelligence officers of Idi Amin's Special Forces. From what I've heard, they are the most cruel of all."

"We appreciate your telling us, Festo," said Archbishop Luwum. "But . . . why are you so concerned about this incident in particular? Unfortunately, thousands of people have disappeared since Idi Amin took control of the country."

"Yes, disappeared—usually under cover of night. But this was broad daylight. They didn't care who saw them. In fact, maybe they wanted people to see and be afraid. Amin is angry . . . and I think I know why." Bishop Kivengere frowned. "It may be just a rumor, but I heard from a reliable source that some army officers attempted a coup last Tuesday. It was squashed right away, and the government is pretending it never happened."

Yacobo sucked in his breath. A coup!

"Last Tuesday?" Theo spoke up. "What's today—February first? That makes last Tuesday . . . January twenty-fifth." He raised his eyebrows. "Oh."

Bishop Kivengere managed a wry grin. "Exactly, Theo. The attempted coup was on January twenty-fifth—the anniversary of Idi Amin's own coup back in '71! I'm sure Amin got the message. But now he'll be more determined to squash anyone he thinks is plotting against him. We . . . well, we must all be 'wise as serpents and harmless as doves,' as the Bible says."

"Thank you, Festo," said the archbishop, clasping his friend's hand. "Don't worry; we'll be careful. God bless you as you and Mera drive back to Kabale."

As the door closed behind Festo Kivengere, Theo took his son aside. "No need to mention this to your mother."

Yacobo nodded, but he wasn't surprised the next morning when his father drove him and Blasio to school and picked them up in the afternoon . . . not only that day but for the rest of the week.

Friday evening Yacobo asked Janini Luwum if he could work awhile on the Centennial play in the archbishop's study. Blasio usually stayed up later on Friday nights, and it was hard to get any studying done in the boys' room. But if Yacobo worked really hard this weekend, he might actually get the first draft done. He'd be glad to get it finished.

The dialogue was coming a little more easily now, and Yacobo wrote page after page. It was after midnight when he laid his head down on his arms and closed his eyes to rest them—just for a minute, he told himself. Somewhere outside he heard a dog start barking, then another one. Then . . . it sounded like someone pounding on a door and shouting.

Yacobo sat bolt upright. That pounding and shouting sounded close—too close.

Suddenly he heard someone hurry past the study door and down the stairs to the front hallway. Opening the study door, Yacobo made his way to the top of

the stairs. He could hear the pounding clearly now on the front door below and shouts of "Archbishop!

Archbishop! Open! We have come!"

Peering down into the hallway from the top of the stairs, Yacobo saw the archbishop in his bathrobe reach the first floor, just as his father rushed into the hallway from the back entrance. Yacobo crept halfway down the stairs and watched as Archbishop Luwum pulled back the curtain on one side of the front door and peered out.

"Oh, I know this man—name's Ben Ongam," the archbishop said. "Looks like he's hurt. Open the door, Theo. Maybe he needs help."

Yacobo watched as his father unlocked the front door and opened it. Suddenly several big men waving pistols pushed a badly frightened man in handcuffs into the entryway and began yelling at the archbishop. "Where are the guns? Show us the guns!"

"What guns?" protested Archbishop Luwum. "There are no guns here."

Yacobo shrank back into the shadows, but where he could still see what was happening. The man the archbishop called Ben Ongam had many cuts and bruises on his face and arms. The other intruders wore colorful casual shirts and carried pistols and rifles. One of the brawny men held a pistol to Theo Kabaza's neck. Another held his rifle on the archbishop while a third searched them both from head to foot.

"We know there are guns here," snapped the leader. "Ongom here confessed that you are fronting for the rebels." The man sneered. "Very smart. No one would think of looking in the archbishop's house, right?" Then he pushed the archbishop so hard that

Janini Luwum nearly fell down. "Walk! Run! Show us the house. We'll find the guns if it takes all night."

Just then one of the armed men saw Yacobo behind the plants. "You!" he yelled, taking three big strides to where Yacobo was crouched. He was a big, muscular man with a flat nose and small eyes. Grabbing Yacobo's arm, he snarled, "Take us to the staff quarters. We'll search there."

Yacobo's legs felt like two wooden sticks, hardly able to obey him. But somehow he led two of the armed men out the back door to the staff quarters.

In the Kabaza apartment, Eunika was anxiously clutching her nightclothes around her. The men ignored her but turned pillows and bedding upside down. In the boys' room, they dumped a startled Blasio out of bed and turned the mattress over. Wide awake now, Blasio watched with wide eyes and open mouth as the armed men searched the room.

The search went on for almost two hours—bedrooms, study, chapel, storerooms, kitchen, courtyard, inside the cars. The men found nothing.

By this time the intruders had rounded up everyone in the main house and staff quarters.

Ben Ongam looked terrified. "Please, Archbishop," he begged, "give me some names of Langi or Acholi families so that these men may search for guns." He didn't say it, but the look in his eyes seemed to say, "It's the only way I know to stay alive."

Yacobo was startled at the mention of the tribal names. Was that what this was all about? He remembered the Kakwa boy at school saying that ex-

79

President Obote, living in exile in Tanzania, was Langi. Maybe Ben Ongam was Langi, too. Langi and Acholi—the Kakwas hated those tribes. Was President Amin afraid some people from those tribes were plotting against him so Obote could regain power?

Yacobo felt a little wave of relief that his family was Bahororo, like the Kivengeres.

"Mr. Ongam," the archbishop was saying, "I am archbishop for all people in Uganda, not just for one or two tribes. This is God's house. There are no guns here. We pray for the president. We pray for the soldiers. We preach the Gospel. We help the poor. That is our work, not smuggling guns."

Janini Luwum turned to the armed men, and his voice changed to steel. "This search of my house in the middle of the night is outrageous! Why not come during the day, with a search warrant in your hand? We have nothing to hide. I am going to tell President Amin of your conduct immediately."

The men simply hardened their faces, pushed Ben Ongam out the door in front of them, and were gone.

No one got any sleep the rest of the night. They put bedding back on the beds, picked up dresser drawers that had been dumped out, straightened up closets and chairs that had been overturned. Finally, Eunika made some tea, and the Kabazas sat around their kitchen table sipping the hot drink silently. Even Blasio had no smart remarks to make.

Suddenly Yacobo wondered something. Turning to his father he said, "Papa, what tribe does Archbishop Luwum come from?"

Theo pursed his lips. "Acholi. Why do you ask?"

Chapter 7

Summoned

YACOBO HAD A HARD TIME concentrating on his lessons at school on Monday. The search of the archbishop's house at gunpoint in the middle of the night had left him shaken and jumpy. Several times his teachers called on him to recite in class, and he stumbled over the answers. Some of the other students snickered. In writing class, Mr. Wabaki said, "You are not paying attention, Yacobo. Is something wrong?" Yacobo just looked at the floor and shook his head.

If only his father would be waiting for him right after school so he could hop in the car and not run into Byensii. But his father's old taxi was not in the school driveway, and Byensii was.

The Kakwa boy held a small transistor radio turned up at its highest volume, and a small crowd of boys was listening intently. Byensii's eyes locked on Yacobo, and he held out the radio. "Listen to this, Christian boy." It was a command, not an invitation.

It took several moments before Yacobo could make out the words on the scratchy transistor radio. Then the announcer's voice became clear. " . . . discovered near the archbishop's house. The schoolchildren alerted the authorities, who quickly confiscated the stash of foreign-made guns. We repeat, several schoolchildren today accidentally discovered a stockpile of weapons near the home of Janini Luwum, the Anglican archbishop. The authorities—"

Yacobo felt a rush of anger flood through him. The so-called "authorities" couldn't find anything during their illegal search in the middle of the night, so now they were making up a story about finding guns *near* the archbishop's house! He felt like yelling, "Lies! Lies! It's all lies!" at the triumphant sneer on Byensii's face. But just then he saw the familiar old taxi pull into the school drive.

Jumping into the front seat, he blurted out to his father what he had just heard. Grim faced, Theo Kabaza quickly drove back to the archbishop's house. Yacobo was surprised to see several bishops from districts all over Uganda standing in the courtyard, talking in twos and threes. One small group was listening to a transistor radio and calling out the news to the others.

"The archbishop has called an emergency council

of the bishops to discuss how to respond to the attack on his home," Theo told Yacobo as he parked the old taxi behind the house. "If they just let it pass, none of the religious leaders in Uganda will be safe from harassment."

All week long the council of bishops met to discuss what to do about this latest outrage by Idi Amin's Special Forces. On Saturday, February 12, most of the bishops returned home, but eight stayed, including Festo Kivengere and Silvanus Wani. Looking tired, but still wearing his warm smile, Bishop Kivengere dropped in to see his friends the Kabazas.

"Mmm, Eunika, you're still one of the best cooks in Uganda," he said, patting his stomach after two generous helpings of her chicken stew. "Yacobo, how is the writing of the play going?"

Yacobo had hoped the bishop might forget to ask. "All right," he said vaguely. "I got the first draft done . . . now my writing teacher will critique it and help me with the second draft."

"Wonderful!" said Bishop Kivengere. "I cannot wait to read it!"

Yacobo squirmed uncomfortably. He wasn't happy with the play. Something was missing . . . yet he didn't know what. But he had to finish the play soon. The Centennial celebration was scheduled for June 1977, less than four months away. Actors had to be chosen, rehearsals gotten underway . . .

The table conversation turned to the week-long council of bishops. "Yes, we prepared another document to present personally to the president, but so far he has refused to see us," sighed Festo. "We reminded the president that many people around the world know me and Archbishop Luwum and are watching Uganda. He cannot abuse our archbishop without reaping worldwide condemnation.

"But the outrageous search of the archbishop's home last weekend is only one of our many concerns. Many of Uganda's best and brightest are fleeing the country, creating a 'brain drain.' Government agents continue to arrest and kill, leaving a distressing number of widows and orphans. Private property and cars are being taken away for military use. The list goes on and on. We will try again early next week to get an appointment with the president to present these concerns in a respectful way, but someone needs to speak up!"

Wasn't it dangerous to speak up? Yacobo thought uneasily. He shivered at what might happen if he challenged Byensii's menacing attitude—and Byensii was only a schoolyard bully, not the president of Uganda.

Someone was knocking on the door. Knocking, knocking . . .

Yacobo sat bolt upright in his bed. A pale gray light coming through his window told him it was early morning. He'd been dreaming about Ben Ongam and the dreaded Special Forces knocking on the archbishop's door. But it wasn't a dream. Someone *was* knocking on the door! His heart seemed to stop. Had Idi Amin's gunmen come back?

But as he listened, he realized the knocking was not at the main house, but on the door of his family's apartment. A familiar voice was calling, "Theo! Theo Kabaza! Are you awake? The archbishop needs you!"

Yacobo could feel his heart begin beating normally again. It was only the archbishop's assistant calling for his father. But what did he want at such an early hour? Yacobo got out of bed and came into the sitting room just as his father, sleepy eyed and unshaven, opened the door.

"Oh, Theo. Sorry to bother you, but the archbishop needs you to drive him and Mary to Entebbe. He needs to be there by nine o'clock this morning."

"Nine o'clock!" Theo said. "We will have to leave right away. What—has something happened?"

The assistant shrugged. "We're not sure. The archbishop got a call late last night from the president . . . very angry, making all sorts of accusations. But the archbishop was able to speak in a firm, loving way, refuting his charges. Then, early this morning, he received another call from the president's office, summoning him to the State House in Entebbe by nine o'clock! Mary is insisting on going with her husband."

"I'll be out front in ten minutes," Theo said as he pulled out a clean shirt. "Yacobo, you will have to take Blasio to school today. Just . . . be careful, son."

Blasio grumbled about not getting a ride, but otherwise seemed oblivious to the general tension in the household caused by the events of the past week. Yacobo knew his mother was anxious about the boys' having to walk to school, but all she said as she handed them their lunches was, "Blasio, you stay with Yacobo, you hear? I'll pick you up after school. And, Yacobo, you be sure to come straight home."

Yacobo intended to duck out of school the moment the school day ended, but Mr. Wabaki asked him to stay after class to talk about his play. The writing teacher had finished his critique and wanted to go over his suggestions with Yacobo.

At least Byensii was nowhere to be seen when Yacobo finally scurried out the door and ran two blocks to catch a matatu. All the way home he wondered what had happened at the State House in Entebbe that day. Would the Luwums and his father be home yet?

To his relief, the official black car was sitting in the driveway when he walked through the gate, along with the Kivengeres' car. Inside the main house, his mother was serving an early tea in the sitting room to everyone, but she grabbed him as he came in. "Where have you been?" she hissed. "I don't need to be worrying about you, too."

"I'm sorry, Mama. I couldn't help it," he whispered back defensively, showing the play with the teacher's handwriting all over it. He pulled away from her and walked over to where his father, the Luwums, and the Kivengeres were just sitting down with their tea and sandwiches. Blasio, as usual, escaping the watchful eye of his mother, was already wolfing down slices of sweet bread.

"It was the strangest thing, Festo," Janini Luwum was saying. "After the president's angry midnight call, I have to admit I was worried what this 'summons' was about. I didn't want Mary to go with me, but she insisted. But when we got there, Idi Amin was laughing and smiling and welcomed us like old friends! He introduced us to his other guest, a Major Greene from England, who had trained Amin as a young army officer. Newspaper reporters were there and took our pictures all together."

Festo Kivengere frowned. "Ah. Now it all makes sense. A friend of mine in London called over the weekend to see if we were all right. It seems British newspapers had published a story that Archbishop Luwum had been arrested and beaten."

Mary Luwum gasped. "You mean, this was just a big show to prove the 'rumors' are false?"

"Yes. But that's not all bad." Bishop Kivengere smiled encouragingly. "Now Amin knows the world is watching."

"Well, I'm afraid I could not let my opportunity go by," said the archbishop. "After Major Greene left, I spoke to the president and protested the search of my house—not the search itself, but *how* it was done, at midnight, at gunpoint. I told the president I had nothing to hide and would gladly cooperate with authorities when done in the proper manner. Then I told Amin that the bishops had been wanting to speak with him all week."

Festo Kivengere lifted his eyebrows. "How did he respond?"

"He laughed loudly and said in his booming voice, 'Don't worry about a thing! I'm going to invite all the bishops to come, and put them up in a hotel at my expense, and we'll talk it all over!' So," the archbishop said with a slight smile, "I left him a copy of our document of concerns. Festo, did you—?"

Bishop Kivengere nodded. "Yes. Bishop Wani and I delivered copies to the cabinet ministers and the secretary of the Defense Council today. In person."

Yacobo saw the adults look at one another with glances that were both wary and cautiously optimistic. "Now we must pray," said the archbishop.

"It looks like the president is being true to his word," Theo Kabaza reported to the family Tuesday evening. "All the religious leaders—Protestant, Catholic, and Muslim—have been summoned to the conference center here in Kampala tomorrow morning. Yacobo, you must walk Blasio to school again, as I am needed to drive the archbishop. I will be gone all day."

"Mm-hmm," Yacobo said absently. He chewed on his pencil and frowned at Mr. Wabaki's comments written in the margins of his play. *WHY would they choose death rather than their own safety?* the teacher had scrawled. *You haven't shown me WHY their faith is that important. Convince me!*

What does he want? Yacobo thought in frustration. *I wrote what the martyrs said. Isn't that enough?*

He read and reread what he'd written and mulled it over in his mind all the next day. Once or twice on Wednesday he wondered what was happening at the meeting with the president that day, but he wasn't too concerned. His father and the Luwums had come home safely from the State House on Monday. Surely nothing would happen today with so many religious leaders present.

After school, he and Blasio settled down to doing their homework in the archbishop's kitchen while Eunika prepared the evening meal for the Luwums and their guests. Mera Kivengere, who was sick with bronchitis, was resting in one of the guest rooms while they waited for the bishops to return.

About five-thirty, Theo Kabaza rushed into the kitchen, his tie loosened, his face damp with sweat. "Eunika, come quickly," he said. "You must go to Mrs. Luwum. The archbishop has been arrested!"

Yacobo followed as his parents rushed to the little chapel where Festo Kivengere and the other seven bishops who had accompanied the archbishop that day were gathered around Mary Luwum. Yacobo caught bits and pieces of the story as Bishop Kivengere tried to tell the archbishop's wife what had happened that day.

They were made to stand outside in the hot sun all day, he said, while the vice-president made angry speeches to a large crowd of army personnel and diplomats. "He accused us of hiding behind our clergy

collars and prayer books while plotting against the
president," said Festo. On cue the soldiers yelled,
"Kill them! Kill them!" Finally, at two o'clock the

religious leaders and diplomats were told to go into the conference center, where they would meet with the president. But the bishops were led into a separate room and kept there while the president addressed everyone else.

"We did not know what was happening in the other room, though we could hear clapping and shouts," said Festo wearily. "Then about three-thirty the meeting was over, and we were bluntly told we could all go home. We were disappointed that we had not been able to meet with the president as expected, but were relieved to go home. As we started to leave, a guard said, 'Not you, Archbishop. The president wants to see you.'"

The other bishops protested. They did not want to leave without their archbishop. They tried to wait but were ordered outside. They waited outside by the car, but still the archbishop did not come out. "Theo here got very stubborn," said Festo. "He said he was the archbishop's driver and would not leave without him. But the guards said they would bring the archbishop home in another car and ordered us at gunpoint to leave. That . . ." his voice nearly broke. "That was when we knew in our hearts that our archbishop had been arrested."

Mary Luwum was weeping. "I must go to the conference center and find out what has happened to my husband," she said suddenly. "Theo, will you please drive me?"

"No, Mrs. Luwum!" said Eunika, holding the other woman. "It is too dangerous."

Bishop Kivengere and the other bishops also tried to discourage her, but Mary Luwum was determined to go. Theo Kabaza said nothing, but put on his hat and went to get the car.

Yacobo knew his father, too, wanted to go back to the conference center. He would not rest until he had done his duty and brought the archbishop back home.

All thoughts of supper and homework were forgotten as everyone stayed in the chapel and prayed. A few hours later, Mary Luwum and Theo Kabaza returned home, their strained faces telling the story. No word about the archbishop.

It was late. Eunika told Yacobo to take Blasio back to their apartment and put him to bed. "I will come get you if we hear anything," she promised.

Yacobo nodded and herded Blasio outside. Once in bed, the younger boy fell asleep right away, but Yacobo lay awake for a long time, listening to the loud silence.

The morning sun was streaming through the bedroom window when Yacobo awoke. At first he was confused. Why had no one awakened him for school? And then he remembered. The archbishop.

Blasio was still sleeping, but his parents' bed had not been slept in. Yacobo pulled on his clothes and went into the back door of the main house in his bare feet. The smell of coffee filled the house. As he passed the open front door, he saw his mother outside in her apron picking up the morning newspaper. He had the eerie feeling that it was just another morning. Maybe the archbishop had been released in the night and everything was all right. But, no, his mother had said she would come tell him if they heard any news.

He cracked the door to the chapel and slipped inside. The bishops were still on their knees, praying. He could see his father among them, his head in his hands. A cough caught his ear. Mera Kivengere was up and dressed, sitting with Mary Luwum, a raspy cough from her chest punctuating the murmured prayers from time to time. But her lips were moving, too, in silent prayer.

Just then a cry of agony tore the quiet fabric of the morning, and Eunika Kabaza ran into the chapel holding the morning newspaper in front of her. The bishops scrambled to their feet as the bold headline leaped out at them:

ARCHBISHOP KILLED IN CAR CRASH

A picture of a wrecked automobile was splashed across the front page.

A moan like a wounded cat escaped the lips of Mary Luwum, and she slumped against Mera Kivengere. But Theo Kabaza took several long strides and snatched the newspaper from his wife. "Let me see that picture." His eyes narrowed. "I recognize that car. It was totaled in a wreck two weeks ago. If our archbishop is dead, he did not die in that car accident."

Chapter 8

Flight

T HEY HAVE MURDERED HIM," said Festo Kivengere quietly, speaking all their thoughts aloud, "and now they are trying to cover it up."

Mary Luwum had slumped to the floor, and Mera Kivengere and Eunika Kabaza were kneeling with her, holding her, and crying with her. Even the grown men were fighting back tears of grief and anger.

Yacobo sank into one of the small pews of the chapel. His eyes burned, and a lump filled his throat. What was happening? Why would anyone kill the kind archbishop? This was crazy! The whole world seemed to be spinning out of control, like a tor- nado that only looks threatening from a distance, and then suddenly is upon you, tearing everything up by its roots.

Suddenly Bishop Kivengere began to sing, a song of hope and trust in Jesus. One by one several of the others joined him, their voices weak, almost whispering. But gradually the voices grew stronger until the last verse faded away.

"Brothers and sisters," said Bishop Kivengere, his own voice husky and breaking with grief, "this is a moment of severe testing. We will be tempted to hate, to want revenge. We may want to fight with whatever power we have available to us to bring this evil man down. But let us remember, the only place of power is down low, at the feet of Jesus. Let us never take our eyes off Him and the reconciling work of the Cross, or we will sink into the waves of destruction that are all around us."

Together the little group cried and prayed. Then they pulled themselves together and tried to decide what to do.

"We must go to the government and ask for Janini's body."

"We must notify the bishops in every district in Uganda—"

"—and friends and officials worldwide."

"We must make arrangements for an official funeral at the Namirembe Cathedral. What day is today? Thursday? Sunday is three days away—February twentieth. Can we do that?"

It was decided that Theo would drive Mrs. Luwum, Bishop Kivengere, and Bishop Wani—who was from the Kakwa tribe, which might be useful—to obtain the body, while others began making the necessary funeral arrangements. Mera Kivengere, who was coughing badly, went to bed, and Eunika Kabaza began cooking pots of food to feed the constant stream of guests that were expected.

Faisi got word at the university, and she and Charity Kivengere came as quickly as they could to help out. Yacobo was saddled with keeping an eye on Blasio, running errands, and taking messages back and forth in the big house.

It was good to keep busy, to put off having to think about what was going to happen after Sunday. But when Theo Kabaza came home that evening, he shook his head in discouragement when his wife asked what happened. "We kept getting the runaround. The minister of health told Mrs. Luwum the matter had been turned over to the minister of defense, and the body would be released after they finished their investigation."

But on Friday, after being sent from official to official, Mrs. Luwum was finally told that her husband's body had already been taken to the archbishop's "home village" in the north and buried. There would be no official funeral in Kampala.

Frustration spilled over as the bishops and staff gathered together Friday night around Mary Luwum. "It's obvious what has happened," Yacobo's father was saying bitterly as the boy slipped into the room. "They do not dare release the body for public burial because he was shot, and that would make a lie out of the car accident story."

"What about the funeral?" Bishop Wani asked.

All looked at Mary Luwum. Tears shone in her eyes as she said bravely, "What is to stop us from celebrating the life of Janini Luwum on Sunday morning at the cathedral—with or without my husband's body?"

Just then Faisi stuck her head in the door. "There are some people at the door. They say they are a delegation from the archbishop's home district and have come to escort Mrs. Luwum home to attend her husband's funeral there."

All eyes looked at Mary Luwum. "I will not go!" she cried. "The government is trying to hush this up, to keep it quiet and private."

"She is right," said Festo Kivengere. "I fear for Mary's safety on the road." Everyone agreed. Bishop Kivengere went out to meet with the delegation and express Mrs. Luwum's regrets.

While he was out of the room, Theo spoke up. "Mrs. Luwum is not the only one whose safety we should be concerned about. While we were out today, we met more than one person who was shocked to see Bishop Kivengere alive and well. There are rumors going around that he, too, has been killed."

"Of course, Festo just smiles and says, 'Well, as you can see, I am quite well, thank you,'" said Bishop Wani. Everyone laughed nervously.

Talk turned once more to plans for the memorial on Sunday. Wandering back to the Kabaza apartment, Yacobo flopped down on his bed, resting his hands behind his head and staring into the darkness outside the small window.

In the quietness, Yacobo let his mind drift beyond the memorial service on Sunday. Who would be the new archbishop? The thought startled Yacobo. What if the new archbishop didn't want his father to be his personal driver? Or his mother to be the cook?

For the first time since the archbishop had been killed, Yacobo suddenly realized his parents' jobs, their home here in Kampala, and his schooling could be gone in a matter of days.

But just as quickly, a comforting idea calmed his anxious thoughts. The new archbishop might be Festo Kivengere. Why not? He was even better known than Janini Luwum had been. Wasn't he an international evangelist? He'd been a close friend and adviser of Archbishop Luwum. They often shared the platform at conventions—two popular preachers. Of course! It made perfect sense. And if Festo Kivengere became archbishop, of course he would want the Kabazas to continue on as part of his household staff. Coming here had been his idea in the first place! And Bishop Kivengere was strong and confident. As long as their bishop friend was there to lead, Yacobo felt safe.

Comforted by these thoughts, Yacobo let his heavy eyelids droop and soon fell into a dreamless sleep.

As Yacobo was getting dressed the next morning—Saturday—he noticed the Centennial play and the rest of his school books sitting on the little desk in the bedroom, untouched since Wednesday night when they first got the news that the archbishop had been arrested. He and Blasio had missed two days of school, and his parents had said nothing about it. Yacobo shrugged. Surely his parents would write an excuse and he could catch up next week.

Blasio, tired of being ignored in the crisis, put salt in Faisi's morning tea and giggled with delight when she gagged and spit it out. He kept bugging his mother until finally she ordered Yacobo to take his brother outside and kick a soccer ball in the driveway until lunch was ready.

People were coming and going all morning. Yacobo sensed something was up. Everyone was talking in low voices, looking worried, and shaking their heads. His mother had left lunch on the table in their apartment for him and Blasio, but the apartment was empty. Then Faisi came in. "Come on over to the chapel right away. Bishop Kivengere wants to talk to everybody."

Curious, Yacobo dragged a reluctant Blasio with him over to the chapel in the main house and made him sit. Seeing that everyone had gathered, Festo Kivengere said, "I have asked you all here to pray with Mera and me as we make a difficult decision. We have received a strong warning that my name is now at the top of Idi Amin's hit list. Several of my brother bishops feel that we need to leave Kampala immediately—maybe even leave the country."

Yacobo sucked in his breath. Leave Uganda?

"I am not inclined to run," Festo continued. "I love my country and am not afraid to die for it. But I must consider seriously what my brothers are saying. They have reminded me of the apostle Paul, who was warned of danger by his friends and let down the city wall so he could get away."

Bishop Kivengere's sober words were interrupted by his wife's raspy cough. He laid a tender hand on her shoulder. "As you can hear, Mera is not well. She is running a fever. We are not sure what to do. We need you to pray with us."

There were murmurs around the room. "God help us." "Have mercy, O God." The murmurs swelled into prayers. Some people knelt; others wept. Even Blasio sat quietly as though pinned to his seat by the urgency of the situation.

And then there was a stillness, and in the stillness Yacobo heard his father say in a voice thick with emotion, "Brother Festo, hear me as one of the people. We have already lost one bishop this week. We cannot afford to lose another one. Please, leave Kampala *now*."

The prayer meeting was interrupted by a phone call for Bishop Kivengere. It was Leighton Ford, American evangelist and son-in-law of Billy Graham, calling to say that many people around the world were concerned about his safety. Another call was put through from Stanley Mooneyham from World Vision with the same concern.

Bishop Silvanus Wani spoke up. "I think God is

making it clear. You and Mera must leave right away—
at least get out of Kampala and go home to Kabale."

And so it was decided. Festo and Mera would
drive home immediately to Kabale. They would test
the situation there as to whether they should stay or
keep going. Theo and Eunika Kabaza offered to drive
behind them so they wouldn't be making the six-
hour trip alone.

And then they were gone.

The entire household waited anxiously for news

all that afternoon and evening. It was late when the telephone rang. Bishop Wani answered it in the archbishop's study. "That was Theo," he reported. "He said it was not safe in Kabale. They are gone."

Gone! That meant Festo and Mera Kivengere were fleeing the country.

As the household finally retired, Yacobo retreated to the bedroom he shared with Blasio in the staff quarters. His younger brother was already asleep in sprawled innocence. Yacobo shook his head. Life swirled around Blasio without seeming to affect him. Yacobo, on the other hand, did not understand all the feelings that churned inside him. Of course he didn't want anything to happen to Bishop Kivengere. Maybe fleeing was the right thing. But stabs of resentment poked holes in those logical thoughts. *What about the rest of us?* Now that Archbishop Luwum was dead, who was going to stand up against the violence and terror if Bishop Kivengere wasn't even in the country? And if Bishop Kivengere wasn't there to be archbishop, who cared whether his parents had a job or Yacobo continued with his writing?

He felt abandoned. Suddenly his eyes fell on the pages of the play script. In one vicious motion, he ripped the pages from top to bottom. Then he wadded them up and threw them in the wastebasket.

Why not? he thought angrily. How could he write now with his world falling apart? Besides, with the archbishop dead and Festo Kivengere fleeing the country, surely there would be no Centennial celebration now.

Chapter 9

Kidnapped

Sometime during the night, Theo and Eunika Kabaza arrived home. After a few hours' sleep, they got washed and dressed and together with Faisi, Yacobo, and Blasio drove to Namirembe Cathedral for the memorial service for Janini Luwum.

The government had announced there would be no official funeral, only "private services." Foreign dignitaries who had wanted to come were refused entrance into the country "for reasons of national security," so the government said. But over 4,500 Ugandans showed up at the Cathedral anyway, and there was nothing the soldiers could do about it.

The former archbishop of

Uganda, Erica Sabiti, who had retired, read the Resurrection story from the New Testament: "'He is not here; he is risen!' All glory to Christ!" The choir started singing, "Glory, glory to the Lamb . . ." The people joined in, and the song swelled in the Cathedral. Yacobo's neck prickled. They were singing, "Tukutendereza Yesu!"—the "Martyrs' Song."

Back home over a simple lunch, Theo and Eunika Kabaza finally had a chance to tell their children what had happened when they got to Kabale. "Neighbors met us at the Kivengeres' house," Theo said, "to tell us that soldiers had come knocking on the door three times that day to see if Festo was home. 'You must go—now!' they said." Mera was still running a fever, but after a brief time of prayer together, Festo and Mera put their suitcases back in the car and, without stopping to take any of their personal things from the house, drove toward the Rwandan border.

"So we don't know if they are safe yet?" Faisi said.

Eunika shook her head. "No. We must keep them in our prayers." She looked anxiously at her daughter. "What about you—are you going back to the university?"

Faisi nodded. "Charity Kivengere will be taking final exams soon. We both want to keep attending classes as long as possible."

To Yacobo's surprise, his father agreed. "You are right. We must keep our chins up and go forward."

A week went by with no news. But rumors were flying of new killings, especially among the Acholi and Langi tribes. Several more bishops fled the country.

And then one day Bishop Wani came to the archbishop's residence with news: Festo and Mera had arrived safely in Nairobi, Kenya!

"The night they left Kabale was very harrowing," said Bishop Wani to the small group who gathered in the little chapel. "People on the road warned them of a roadblock up ahead, so they drove the car through the forest with the headlights off until they got around it. A while later they had to abandon the car and go the last distance into Rwanda by foot, up the mountains. It was very difficult for Mera, who was still feverish and wearing a long skirt. But just at sunrise on Sunday, February twentieth, the day of the archbishop's memorial service, they crossed the border into Rwanda, singing praises to God."

Yacobo felt something in his chest relax, like a tightly wound spring unwinding. He was glad the Kivengeres were safe. But the fact that they left at all was still a sore point.

Bishop Wani had other news. "I had a long talk with Festo," he said. "He encouraged us—and I agree—to continue with the plans for the Centennial celebration in June." The bishop put up his hand as several people started to protest. "If we don't, brothers and sisters, then 'Big Daddy' Amin has already won. But as our brother Festo said, the celebration of God's work in Uganda must go on!"

Yacobo felt a stab of panic. If the Centennial celebration was still going to happen, that meant—

Bishop Wani was speaking directly to him. "Bishop Kivengere asked how your script was coming along, Yacobo. He said when you have finished, he would like to see a copy!"

Yacobo swallowed. He thought of the script, torn in two and thrown into the wastebasket. Was it even still there? Or had it been taken out to the dustbin?

Guiltily he slipped out of the chapel and ran back to his apartment. The wastebasket in the boys' bedroom was overflowing. Dumping it upside down, he pawed through the scrunched-up school papers, rotting melon rinds, banana peels, and pencil shavings.

The script was still there—ripped, wadded up, and dirty. Yacobo let out a long breath of relief.

Yacobo stayed up most of that night taping together the damaged script and then recopying it onto clean paper. As he recopied, he started rewriting, working on the second draft.

Day after day, he worked on rewriting the play. He focused on the notes his teacher had written in the margins. *Too stiff. Would someone really talk this way?* or *More feeling! The king is really angry!* He felt driven to get it done. Bishop Wani had said rehearsals would begin as soon as school break began. At the same time, Yacobo felt as though he was forcing his writing, like rolling rocks uphill.

It didn't help that the rumors of more arrests and killings were growing. What kind of country makes war on its own people! The whole world seemed crazy. Yacobo shut his ears and tried to block it all out.

It might have worked—except for Byensii. The first week Yacobo returned to school after the archbishop's murder, Byensii backed him up against a wall and sneered, "That traitor Luwum had it coming!"

"You don't know what you're talking about!" Yacobo screamed and pushed himself past Byensii, hearing the other boy's laughter behind him.

As the body count on the radio and in the newspapers grew, the Kakwa boy strutted and crowed about "rooting out the rebels." Fistfights in the hallways and athletic field became common, usually Kakwa boys picking fights with Acholi or Langi students. Yacobo did his best to steer clear of Byensii, but his anger at the other boy grew hard and bitter. "One of these days . . ." he muttered to himself, relishing fantasies of making Byensii eat his words.

Finally he finished his rewrite of the play. With a few corrections here and there, Mr. Wabaki pronounced it "Good," and said he looked forward to seeing it performed at the Centennial celebration in June.

Good? Yacobo thought as he walked out of the school. He had hoped his writing teacher would be impressed, that he'd say, "Excellent!" or "Wonderful!" But Yacobo had to admit to himself that even he wasn't totally satisfied with the job he'd done on the play. Maybe "Good" was a fair evaluation.

"What's this?" said a dreaded voice. Yacobo felt the play script being snatched from his hand.

"Give that back!" yelled Yacobo, grabbing for the papers that Byensii was now holding.

" 'Martyrs' Song," by Yacobo Kabaza,' " Byensii

read in a mocking voice. He scanned through several pages, jerking them out of reach as Yacobo tried to get them back. "What is this? A crybaby tale of boys like you, too stupid to know they've been duped by white people's religion? This is just a bunch of trash!"

Panic rushed through Yacobo's veins. That was the only copy of the play he had! He could never write it again! Pushing and punching, he grabbed wildly for the papers in the older boy's hands, but Byensii just laughed and dangled them out of reach. Finally, with a desperate leap, Yacobo grabbed the papers and took off running, Byensii's mocking laughter chasing after him.

He apologized to Bishop Wani for the wrinkled pages, but the bishop told him he would have his assistant type up the script and make several copies.

Bishop Wani was filling in for the archbishop until a new one was appointed. Mrs. Luwum was getting ready to move, but the Kabazas had been asked to stay on to help in the transition.

"I'm glad Blasio has something to do during the school holiday," Eunika Kabaza said when Bishop Wani told her rehearsals for the Centennial play would be held at the cathedral twice a week for six weeks during April and May. "That boy has more energy than a wind-up toy!"

It became Yacobo's job to take Blasio to and from the cathedral for rehearsals. But Eunika was very worried about the boys' safety. "Keep to the main street," she told Yacobo. "Don't take any shortcuts. Avoid attracting the attention of any soldiers. And don't let Blasio out of your sight!"

Five boys of different ages had been selected to complete the acting troupe for a total of six, some playing more than one role. The director spent the first few rehearsals assigning roles and hearing the boys read through their lines. Yacobo quickly became bored. After all, he knew the script backward and forward. He might as well do something else until it was time to pick Blasio up and take him home.

After wandering the streets around the cathedral during a few rehearsals, Yacobo tried something a little more daring: He caught a matatu to the university, slipped into the library, and browsed the books and magazines before catching another matatu back to Namirembe Hill. By timing how long it took to travel to and from the university, Yacobo discovered he had about one hour free to read in the library in order to get back to the cathedral in time to pick up his younger brother.

Only one hour was like biting into a juicy mango and having to stop at one bite. Yacobo found himself devouring travel books on South Africa, Nigeria, Australia, Russia. References in these books sent him looking for other books on other subjects: the Boer War in South Africa; the practice of banishing English criminals to Botany Bay, the prison colony in Australia; stories by the Russian writer Leo Tolstoy. . . He was frustrated at not being able to check out any books to read at home and eagerly looked forward to his private journeys into other times and places.

One day his mother received a letter from Mera Kivengere in Pasadena, California, which Eunika read aloud to the family at the supper table. "She says Festo travels a good deal, preaching and trying to arouse concern about the situation here in Uganda. He is also trying to organize something to help the thousands of refugees fleeing into other African countries. . . . Oh, she is very frightened for Charity at the university and wants us to beg her to leave and go stay with her sister Peace." Eunika looked up. "Theo, do you think we should insist that Faisi leave, too, before something terrible happens?"

Yacobo had heard this conversation a dozen times.

In spite of the growing tensions in the capital city, plans for the Centennial celebration marched forward. To no one's surprise, Bishop Silvanus Wani was appointed the next archbishop of the Church of Uganda. Yacobo shrugged off his disappointment. He had hoped it would be Festo Kivengere, but it served him right for leaving the country.

Dress rehearsals for the Centennial play loomed the last week of May. "Please stay and watch the dress rehearsals!" Blasio begged Yacobo. "I've got my lines all memorized, and you can see what a good job I'm doing as Yusufu."

"Why would I want to see the dress rehearsals?" Yacobo said crossly. Seeing the disappointed look on Blasio's face, he softened a little. "I'm sure you're doing a good job, Blasio. But I want to see the real performance, kind of like for the first time."

Riding the matatu to the university, Yacobo realized he was feeling more and more anxious about seeing the play. Why? It made him feel naked having his writing be exhibited to a lot of people in this way. What if they thought the writing wasn't very good? And then there was the whole thing about Blasio playing the part of Yusufu. He wished it were a stranger, somebody he didn't know.

Yacobo shrugged off the feeling and enjoyed the extra time he got to spend in the university library. Dress rehearsals were longer than usual; he had plenty of time to get back and pick up Blasio. By the time the matatu dropped him off near Namirembe Cathedral, his stomach was complaining, and he hurried to get Blasio so they could go home for supper.

But as he turned the corner, he stopped. One . . . no, two black Mercedes were pulled up in front of the cathedral. They were the kind of cars government men rode in. In spite of the mild seventy-degree weather, chills ran up Yacobo's back. Was something wrong? Should he run in to see if something was the matter? Should he—

Just then the door of the cathedral burst open, and a man in sunglasses and a brightly colored shirt stepped outside. He was holding an automatic weapon and stood guard right outside the door. Yacobo ducked down behind a parked car and peeked around the taillight. Right behind the guard, more men wearing sunglasses and carrying pistols hustled down the steps, pushing several boys ahead of them

111

toward the black cars. The boys said nothing, but the terrified looks on their faces said everything.

Blasio! Those men had Blasio! Why were Idi Amin's henchmen taking the boys from the acting troupe? Yacobo wanted to scream for help, but his whole body felt paralyzed as he watched the men push all six boys into two of the cars. Car doors slammed, tires squealed, and the black cars roared down the hill and out of sight.

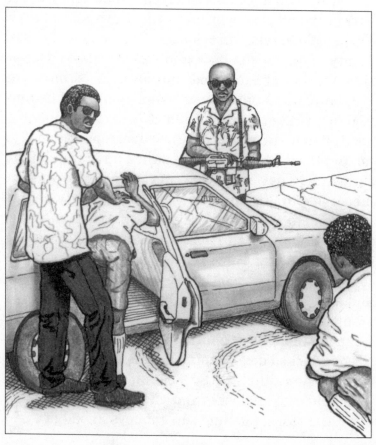

Chapter 10

Winds of Fire

AFTERWARD, Yacobo couldn't even remember how he got back home, or what he said when he stumbled, gasping for breath, into the apartment. But he would never forget the look of fear on his mother's face, like that of an antelope cornered by hungry lions.

"Blasio!" she whispered in a strangled voice. "They took Blasio?" And then her voice became louder and louder, until it was almost a scream. "Why did they take my baby? Where is he? *I've got to find him!* I've got to find—"

Suddenly she turned on Yacobo. "Where were you, boy?" she demanded. "You were supposed to take care of Blasio! Where were you?"

Yacobo tried to swallow, but his mouth was as dry as week-old bread. "I . . . I was just coming back to pick him up," he said miserably.

"Back from where?" his mother screamed.

"Eunika! Not now, not now," Theo Kabaza interrupted, taking his wife by the shoulders and turning her face to look at him. "Yacobo could not have stopped those men. They might have taken him, too! We've got to pull ourselves together and find Blasio. I'm going to go get help. You must contact Faisi at the university, tell her to come home. Pray! We must pray."

Theo jammed his cap on his head and rushed out.

Yacobo's mother just sat in a chair and rocked herself, moaning, "Oh, God, they've taken my baby. Oh, God . . ."

Not knowing what else to do, Yacobo used the archbishop's phone to call Faisi at the residence hall at Makerere University. She wasn't there, so he left a message at the front desk.

Waiting was hard. Too much time to think. Why would Idi Amin's Special Forces kidnap six boys? Surely the president didn't think they were plotting to overthrow the government! Ridiculous!

Faisi flew into the staff quarters about ten o'clock that night. She made Yacobo tell what happened. When Yacobo confessed that he'd been at the university library reading, he saw his mother's eyes flash anger again, but she turned away and didn't say anything.

"Come on, now, Mama," Faisi said in a steady voice, "let's pray. We must pray. God is bigger than this. Come on, now . . ."

They prayed—or rather, Faisi did. All Yacobo could manage was a desperate silent plea. *O Jesus, please help Taata find Blasio, and make him be all right.*

They waited all through the night with no word. Morning came, and Faisi fixed tea for everyone and buttered some bread. Then they heard slow footsteps coming up to the door. The door opened and Theo Kabaza just stood there, looking from one to the other and opening his mouth, as though searching for the right words.

Eunika half rose from the kitchen table. "Blasio," she whispered. "Did you find . . . ?"

Theo's shoulders heaved. "Dead," he said in a hollow voice. "The local police found . . . found all six boys dead in a vacant lot."

Dead? Not dead! The words screamed silently inside Yacobo's mind as he lay on his bed, hot tears streaming down his face. In a sudden fit of rage, he beat on his pillow again and again, until he finally fell back in exhaustion.

Why? Why kill six innocent boys? Archbishop Wani said there was only one reason: Idi Amin wanted to stop the church's Centennial celebration. The president felt threatened by the idea of thousands of Christians gathering in Kampala in joyful worship. *He* was master of Uganda. He didn't want anything going on he couldn't control.

In the next room, Yacobo could hear his mother weeping. She'd been crying for hours. He could hear Faisi's voice, alternately crying with her, praying with her, making soothing murmurs.

His mother blamed him. Yacobo knew she did. Why not? He blamed himself. *If only I hadn't gone to the library!* his mind accused. Would Blasio be alive and well right now? Would it have made any difference? He remembered how helpless they had all been the night Amin's gunmen had pushed their way into the archbishop's house. What could he have done against men with guns?

As Yacobo lay on the rumpled bed, the pillow wet with his tears, the "if onlys" kept coming. If only Blasio hadn't been acting in the Centennial play. . . . If only Yacobo hadn't agreed to write the play in the first place! . . . If only plans for the Centennial celebration had been dropped after the archbishop was killed—

Suddenly Yacobo sat up in his bed as a fierce, hot resentment seemed to bore a hole in his gut. If Bishop Kivengere hadn't encouraged them to go ahead with the Centennial play anyway, even after the archbishop had been murdered, Blasio would be alive today.

The next few days felt unreal. Like watching terrible things happen on a movie screen, Yacobo felt distant, detached. His father and Archbishop Wani retrieved Blasio's body from the police. The small coffin sat in the intimate chapel of the archbishop's residence like a stark exhibit in a museum. The family gathered in the chapel with the new archbishop to discuss what should happen next.

"Maybe we should leave Uganda," Theo said, his voice still husky with grief. "My family is too high a price to pay for Amin's madness."

"I just want to bury my boy back home in Kabale," Eunika said dully, her eyes on the coffin.

"There will be a memorial service for all six boys at the cathedral in a few days," said the archbishop kindly.

"I just want to bury my boy back home in Kabale," she repeated.

Theo Kabaza laid an arm around his wife's sagging shoulders and nodded. "She is right. We will go home to Kabale right away—tomorrow."

Faisi nodded slowly. "Yes. I will come, too. But I worry about Charity . . ."

"She is already gone," Archbishop Wani said reassuringly. "Strangers have been reported on campus, asking where she stays, what her schedule is. We all agreed she is not safe at the university. She has gone to stay with her sister Peace, whose married name gives some safety."

School was just about to start after the two-month holiday, but no one said anything about

Yacobo's school. He shrugged to himself. What did he care? It didn't matter. Nothing really mattered anymore.

They buried Blasio next to his grandfather in a Bahororo graveyard on the outskirts of Kabale. "Children shouldn't go before their mothers and grandmothers," wailed Eunika as dirt was shoveled in on top of her son's coffin.

"Do not forget," Theo said gently to his wife, "Blasio is with Jesus. He, too, is a martyr in the kingdom of God."

"Thank you, Jesus!" whispered Faisi fervently.

Yacobo clenched his teeth. A martyr? More like a victim. Where was the triumph, the so-called "ringing testimony" in his brother's death? Slaughtered, that's all. Slaughtered like goats on butchering day.

Maybe all those martyr stories were just myths— made-up stories to give some "meaning" to senseless, tragic deaths like Blasio's. What a fool he'd been to try to write up the martyr stories! No wonder he couldn't make them sound believable.

The Kabazas stayed with Eunika's mother until they found a small bungalow of their own to rent. As the rainy season ended and the June sun warmed the air and kissed the tops of the Bufumbira Mountains in the west, gradually they tried to put their lives back together. Theo got his job back as a taxi driver, and Faisi got a job as a secretary at the

Kigezi district church office, which was trying to hold things together in Bishop Kivengere's absence.

But even though it was the middle of the school year, Yacobo refused to attend the high school. "I won't go," he told his parents flatly. "I'm fifteen, and I don't have to finish. I'll get a job."

Later he heard his parents talking about him—or rather, he heard his father talking to his mother about him. His mother rarely said anything to or about Yacobo anymore. She seemed sunk in her grief, doing household chores mechanically. When Yacobo did catch his mother's eye, he looked away quickly to avoid the blame he saw there.

"I have a friend—Michael Barongo, remember him?—who farms not far from town," said Theo to his wife. "He said he'd take Yacobo on. It's a hard time for the boy. Some physical labor will probably be good for him." But there was sadness in his voice.

Fine, thought Yacobo. *That's exactly what I want.*

Theo fixed up an old bicycle for Yacobo to use to get back and forth to work on Mr. Barongo's farm. Yacobo went early and came home late, eating the cold supper his mother left for him. And soon it became easier to just stay overnight most nights during the week and come home only on weekends.

Yacobo liked the hard work—once the blisters on his hands healed and formed calluses. He hoed potatoes, yams, carrots, onions, and cabbage. He fed goats and mucked out sheds. He learned how to milk the Longhorn cows, leaning into their soft, warm sides and hearing the milk *swish, swish* into the metal bucket. Mr. Barongo, silver-haired, with smile wrinkles around his eyes, told Yacobo that their tribespeople, the Bahororos, traditionally were cow herders. Cows were valued and respected, and the rhythms of the day revolved around milking and herding. As a child in his family kraal, the farmer told Yacobo, he drank nothing but milk mixed with cow's blood until the age of fourteen.

Yacobo wasn't sure about milk and cow's blood, but he was glad to be on Mr. Barongo's farm. It was hard work, but he liked it that way. It made him tired—too tired to think at night when he fell into bed.

One weekend when he was home, Faisi said, "We got a letter from Bishop Kivengere—there on the table if you want to read it."

Yacobo ignored it. But as he was about to leave for work early Monday morning, he casually picked up the letter and skimmed through it. News of the tragic deaths of the young actors had reached them in America, the bishop wrote, and he and Mera grieved deeply with their friends. *Please, dear friends,* the letter said, *do not let the terrible loss of your beloved son keep you from receiving the deep love of Christ and giving that love to others. It is the love of Christ that heals wounded hearts. Love is a language anyone can understand.*

A fresh flood of resentment broke through the wall of apathy Yacobo had built over the last few months. He threw the letter aside. Love! Could love bring Blasio back? Could love fill his mother's empty arms again? He slammed the door of the bungalow, hopped on his bicycle, and pedaled furiously toward Mr. Barongo's farm.

The new school year rolled around in January of 1978, and still Yacobo refused to go to school. But since he was still willing to work on Mr. Barongo's farm, his parents let him continue. Eunika gradually came out of her shell, but still she and Yacobo talked very little, and they never talked about Blasio.

In June, a year after he started working for Mr. Barongo, the aging farmer gave Yacobo a small, unused garden plot of his own to plant, and said he could take home or sell all the produce. Yacobo, now sixteen, worked feverishly, tilling the ground behind a plodding cow, planting seeds, chopping out weeds, watching with satisfaction as the little shoots of yams and potatoes and corn pushed up through the rich red earth. He daydreamed about taking home the first bushel of vegetables that he'd grown himself and imagined a big smile on his mother's face.

At home he said nothing about the garden plot Mr. Barongo had given him. Faisi was enjoying her job at the district church office and often brought home reports of Bishop Kivengere's travels. He had set up an organization to help Ugandan refugees and get them resettled in Tanzania, Kenya, Rwanda, and Burundi, with aid from Christians around the world. "He hasn't lost his sense of humor," Faisi laughed once, reading a news report from England. "Some reporter asked him if Idi Amin refused to let him back in the country. 'No,' Festo grinned, 'he just couldn't guarantee my safety!' "

Yacobo did not join in the general laughter.

In October, the newspapers trumpeted that General Amin was taking a "bold new offensive" against Tanzania, where Milton Obote was living in exile. But the invasion fizzled out, and the *Monitor* and other newspapers skillfully refocused the public's attention on the fires sweeping across African grasslands, threatening wildlife and farmers' crops.

Pedaling his bicycle along the tarred road toward the farm, Yacobo shut out the news of an invasion, just like he shut out the reports of continued slaughter among the northern tribes of Uganda. All he cared about right now was doing his work for Mr. Barongo and harvesting the vegetables he'd planted before the fall rainy season set in. He pushed hard against the pedals as the road eased up a long, low hill. He was not really thinking, not really seeing the gray-black haze that was boiling up over the horizon.

But as he crested the hill and started to coast down toward the farm, he was startled to see smoke like boiling clouds rolling along the ground under a clear blue sky. He pulled up on his bicycle and stared for a moment. Then he realized what he was looking at: *grass fire!* And it was sweeping straight toward Mr. Barongo's farm!

Chapter 11

Stronger Than Hate

YACOBO STOOD AT THE EDGE of the garden he'd planted and nudged a charred cornstalk with his boot. The entire plot was still smoking from the fire that had raged two days earlier. In fact, as far as his eye could see, the land was scorched and blackened.

Mr. Barongo's house and outbuildings had been spared, thanks to a muddy irrigation ditch he had dug years earlier to catch the rains during the rainy seasons. But the crops were gone. The grasslands were gone. Alive, green, and thriving one day, holding so much promise . . . and the next gone, just like that.

Suddenly Yacobo's chest began to heave, and a loud cry of protest sprang from somewhere deep inside him. Dropping to his knees, he put his face in his hands as sobs shook his whole body. The garden—gone. Blasio—gone. Archbishop Luwum—gone. Bishop Kivengere—gone. His writing—gone. Everything—gone, gone, gone.

After losing his fall crops, Mr. Barongo could not afford to pay Yacobo to work for him anymore. Yacobo shrugged. What did it matter? Nothing much mattered anymore. Using his bicycle, he managed to find several odd jobs running errands and making deliveries for Kabale shop owners—anything to help bring some money *into* the house and keep him *out of* the house as much as possible.

The New Year of 1979 was heralded in the newspapers as "the eighth year of President Amin's 'Life Presidency.'" Yacobo tried not to think about the future. What kind of future could it be with Idi Amin as "president for life"? It was still too dangerous in Kampala for Faisi to return to Makerere University. Why should he bother even going to high school if there was no hope of completing his education? Idi Amin had already ruined their lives and was going to ruin the whole country, just like the grass fire had destroyed all the land in its path.

In February, the newspapers reported that Ugandan "rebels" were joining up with the Tanzanian army to invade Uganda. But Idi Amin's government didn't seem too worried. Hadn't they already crushed an earlier attempt by Tanzania to invade Uganda?

Even though his father and sister tried to keep up with the news, Yacobo let it all go in one ear and out the other. The biggest problem he let his mind consider was how to do his delivery job. The spring rains had started early, making it difficult for Yacobo to be out on his bicycle.

One late afternoon, soaked to the skin, he leaned his bicycle against the bungalow and ducked into the house to get dry clothes and a slicker before going back out again. To his surprise, his mother was curled up against some cushions, reading a small blue book. She didn't even look up when he came in, but he noticed a strange, hungry look on her face, as if she was devouring the words on the page. Strange. It had been a long time since his mother had done any reading, not even the Bible.

The next day he saw her reading again, and this time she was crying. Yacobo felt uneasy. What kind of book would make his mother cry? He hadn't seen her cry since Blasio was killed. In fact, all her emotions had seemed to dry up. She looked up and saw him looking at her, and for a moment he thought she was going to speak to him. But her eyes filled with tears again, and she looked away.

Curious, Yacobo waited till his mother left the house to go to market, then he stole a look at the book title: *I Love Idi Amin*. A jolt of anger surged through him. What was this trash? He snatched up the book and looked at the author's name: *Bishop Festo Kivengere*.

Yacobo threw the book across the room. How *dare* Bishop Kivengere write such a book? How could he write about *loving* the man who was responsible for killing his brother? And why would his mother—his *mother*, of all people!—read it?

At supper, Yacobo had to practically bite his tongue to keep from demanding where the book had come from. But he didn't dare lash out in anger at Bishop Kivengere in front of his mother. Didn't she still blame *him* for not staying with Blasio at the cathedral that terrible day?

The tense suppertime was finally over, and Faisi started to clear the dishes from the table. To Yacobo's surprise, his mother said, "Yacobo, could . . . could I talk with you?"

Yacobo stiffened. Talk to him? He and his mother hadn't really talked in almost a year and a half. Was she going to dump all her feelings of blame on him again? Didn't she know nothing could be worse than the blame he already felt for Blasio's death?

The rain had stopped, and Eunika Kabaza walked outside into the damp evening. Yacobo followed obediently, wishing desperately he was someplace else. Standing beside her, Yacobo realized he had grown taller than his mother.

"Yacobo," Eunika said slowly, "this is very hard to say. Because I know you have felt blamed by me for Blasio's death . . ."

Yacobo sucked in his breath painfully. Yes, he had sensed it, felt it. But it was like a sharp knife in his gut to hear her actually say the words.

"But I want you to know that Christ has taken away all blame from my heart. In fact . . ." His mother paused and turned to Yacobo, lifting her eyes to meet his. They were brimming with tears. "In fact, *I was wrong* to blame you, my son. Will you—can you—forgive me for holding you so far away from my heart?"

Yacobo blinked rapidly and tried to swallow the lump in his throat. *No, no!* his mind cried out. *It is I who needs to be forgiven for leaving Blasio at the cathedral without your permission!* But the words would not come out.

As if reading his mind, she said gently, "You were wrong to leave Blasio during the play rehearsals without telling us . . . but your father is right. You could not have stopped those gunmen even if you had been there. *It is not your fault, Yacobo!* I forgive you, and God forgives you. Now . . . you must forgive yourself."

"Oh, Mama," Yacobo whispered, his voice choked. She put her arms around him as mother and son cried together.

After a few minutes, Eunika said softly, "You see, Yacobo, Bishop Kivengere has reminded me that God's love is stronger than hate. If we don't forgive those who have hurt us, we allow them to continue to hurt us every time we think about the evil they have done. But if we forgive others like God forgives us, we break the power of evil in the world. We are free! Free to love again, free to live again." She kissed him and went inside.

Yacobo could hardly sleep that night. What had happened to bring about such a change in his mother? And yet something . . . no, everything seemed different. In the morning he heard her singing and praising God in the kitchen, just like she always used to. And the walls between them had just . . . disappeared. She smiled at him and touched him gently on the shoulder as he sat down to eat his breakfast of boiled millet and mashed bananas.

The rain had started again, heavy now, and

Yacobo could not do his deliveries. Picking up the book by Festo Kivengere, he started to read. It was like walking a familiar road after a long, long time of being away. The little book started by telling the story of the arrest and death of Archbishop Janini Luwum at the beginning of the Centennial year of the Church of Uganda. *How like the beginning of our church this was!* Festo wrote, *when our church started with shed blood. But,* he wrote, *a living church cannot be destroyed by fire or guns.*

Yacobo could not put the little book down. Chapter by chapter Festo Kivengere told the story of Idi Amin's ruthless grasp for power and the events of the past eight years. Each event, so familiar to Yacobo, right up to Festo and Mera Kivengere's flight out of Uganda. But then Bishop Kivengere shared his own struggle in exile, of his heart becoming hard and bitter toward this man, Idi Amin, who had murdered his friend, threatened his daughter, spied on his home, and made it necessary to live in exile apart from his beloved country.

So, Yacobo thought. Festo Kivengere also knew anger and hate.

He kept reading. On Good Friday of that first year in exile, as Bishop Kivengere meditated on the Crucifixion story, he was struck by Jesus' words, "Father, forgive them, for they do not know what they are doing." The bishop asked himself: Could he forgive Idi Amin? The Lord seemed to be saying to him, "You owe Amin the debt of love, for he is one of those for whom Christ shed His precious blood."

Yacobo put the book down. He mulled over Bishop Kivengere's words. God forgave us while we were still sinners . . . Christ forgave people who tortured Him . . . Bishop Kivengere said God wanted him to love Idi Amin . . . his own mother forgave him. . . .

The thoughts overwhelmed him. He had to think.

The April rain had eased to a light mist. Shrugging into a light slicker and hopping on his bicycle, Yacobo began to ride out of the town, out into the countryside. He hadn't been out to Mr. Barongo's farm for several months. It had been too depressing to see the ruined fields. But maybe he should say hello to the old fellow. The fresh air felt good in his lungs, and pedaling the bicycle up and over the gentle hills sent blood surging through his body.

As he neared the farm and came over a small rise, something seemed different. At first Yacobo didn't know what it was. Then suddenly he braked and stood staring at the fields all around him.

Every single field had burst into bloom, lush and green in the gray mist. The charred ground had all but disappeared under new green shoots poking up through the ashes, even thicker than the year before.

Yacobo grinned, then began to laugh. All around him nature was confirming what Bishop Kivengere had been writing about: The fires of destruction may destroy for a time, but God's power is stronger than evil and hate and feeds new life even in the middle of devastation.

When Yacobo finally rode his bicycle back into town, he thought he heard the sound of drums, music, and shouting. *What could that be?* he wondered. It wasn't a holiday, was it? It had started to drizzle again, but everywhere he looked, people were out in the street, dancing in the rain, hugging each other, laughing and shouting.

Quickly riding home, he let the bicycle drop to the ground as he rushed inside. The bungalow was full of neighbors, talking and laughing. "What has happened?" he asked. "Why are people out in the street?"

"What?" Faisi cried. "You haven't heard? The Tanzanian army has entered the city of Kampala, and Idi Amin's own soldiers have turned against him. He has fled the country!"

Finally the last neighbor had gone home and the rest of the family was in bed. But Yacobo sat on his bed, leaning against the wall. Something new was stirring inside him. He kept thinking about Bishop Kivengere's little book. Just words on paper, but they had wakened his mother's sleeping spirit and put things into a new light for him, as well.

Words on paper . . .

With sudden determination, Yacobo reached over to the little table beside his bed, pulled out paper and pencil, and began to write.

Chapter 12

My Weapon Is Love

THE STREETS OF KABALE were full of people in a holiday mood. Drums and flutes added to the merriment as people sang and danced. Today was Saturday, May 12, 1979, and their very own bishop was coming home from exile!

Theo and Eunika Kabaza, followed by Faisi and Yacobo, pushed their way into St. Peter's Cathedral. Kabale's modest cathedral was already packed with men, women, and children eager to see Bishop Kivengere. Everyone was by now familiar with the news: After the Tanzanian army had helped liberate Kampala, Yusufu Lule had been named "interim president"; Idi Amin had fled

133

Uganda and asked for sanctuary in Libya; the so-called "State Research Bureau" had been opened, revealing stockpiles of weapons, torture chambers, and hundreds of rotting corpses.

But Bishop Festo Kivengere's return to the Kigezi district in the southwestern corner of Uganda had become their symbol that Idi Amin's reign of terror was truly broken.

From the cheers of the hundreds outside, Yacobo guessed that the Kivengeres had finally arrived. Soon the beaming bishop and his wife were led into the church, their necks adorned with garlands of flowers. Hands from all sides stretched out toward them as they slowly made their way to the front of the church. Along with the cheers and singing, the whole congregation was clapping. Faisi and Yacobo grinned at each other. They had never heard anyone clap for someone in an Anglican church!

Finally the congregation quieted down so the bishop could speak. His voice choked with emotion, Bishop Kivengere said, "It is a great, great joy—I can't put it into words!—to feel in Uganda the fresh air of liberty, to look around, no guns at one's back." He opened his Bible and read Psalm 126, the psalm of hope that had sustained him all during his exile. . . .

When the LORD turned again the captivity of Zion, we were like them that dream. Then was our mouth filled with laughter, and our tongue with singing: then said they among the heathen, The LORD hath done great things for

134

them. The LORD hath done great things for us; whereof we are glad.

" 'The Lord hath done great things for us, whereof we are glad!' " the bishop repeated. His voice broke and he could hardly continue. But at the end of his greeting, he said, "Uganda has suffered deeply. There are gaping wounds that must be healed. But we cannot afford retaliation and revenge. We cannot reconstruct without reconciliation. The healing love of Jesus Christ is the only antidote to the terror that has poisoned our country. Uganda is not destroyed! Uganda is the land of resurrection!"

Eunika reached over and squeezed Yacobo's hand. He gave his mother a quick smile. It was true. The reconciling love of Jesus had healed his relationship with his mother. But there was still something else he had to do before he was free.

The Kabaza family attended the big feast in Festo and Mera's honor at Kigezi High School that evening. Theo and Eunika Kabaza then went home to bed, but Yacobo and Faisi joined a crowd of neighbors and friends who built a bonfire under the canopy of African stars, and spent the night singing and praying with joy outside the Kivengere home.

Yacobo tried not to be impatient as he watched the sparks from the fire dance and snap. But the way things were going, it might be days before he could speak to Bishop Kivengere alone!

The next day, Sunday, St. Peter's Cathedral was again crowded with well-wishers. Bishop Kivengere addressed the congregation, again encouraging his fellow Ugandans to not give in to bitterness and hate. "While I was in exile," he said, "I was asked how I would react if I were handed a gun and President Amin were sitting opposite me. The only reply that I could give was that I would hand the gun to the president and say: 'I think this is your weapon. It is not mine. My weapon is love.'"

There was a shuffling and murmuring throughout the congregation. Yacobo thought he knew what most people were thinking: *Do I have that kind of love?*

On the way home from the cathedral in the old taxi, Theo Kabaza said thoughtfully, "We must pray that Uganda heeds the words of Bishop Kivengere. Already I have heard people talking about making the Kakwa tribespeople pay for the sins of Idi Amin."

Take revenge on the Kakwas? For the first time in almost two years, Yacobo thought of Byensii, his old enemy at school in Kampala. Was Byensii afraid now? A slight flicker of satisfaction made him want to smile. But then he thought of the bishop's final words that morning: *"I don't believe the church can ever take up the sword to fight and still have a ministry of healing."*

Help me, Jesus! he prayed silently. *Help me love Byensii in my heart.*

The weekend of celebration was over, and the next week Yacobo finally rode his bicycle over to the Kivengere home. He wore a pouch slung across his shoulder.

"Yacobo!" said Bishop Kivengere, greeting him with a big smile. "You have grown into a young man since I last saw you."

Mera Kivengere greeted him with a sad smile. "We were devastated to hear about . . . about Blasio and the other boys."

The bishop and his wife wanted to hear all about his family, but Yacobo finally was able to say, "Bishop Kivengere, I . . . I have something I need to say to you."

Gracefully, Mera Kivengere suddenly thought of something she had to do and excused herself.

Yacobo had thought about this moment for weeks, but now that it was here, he was having a hard time finding the words. Finally he said, "Bishop Kivengere, I need to ask you to forgive me. I . . . I was angry when you left the country after Archbishop Luwum's death. And after Blasio and the other boys acting in the Centennial play were killed, I blamed you for encouraging the bishops to go ahead with the Centennial celebration in spite of the political climate."

Yacobo paused. Festo Kivengere was listening intently, but he did not say a word.

The boy took a deep breath. "But I was wrong in my heart. I know that now. Can you . . . can you forgive me for holding these things against you?"

There. It was out. But what would Bishop Kivengere think? Would he think this was a back-handed way of trying to accuse him?

"Oh, Yacobo," said the bishop kindly. "You and your family have suffered so much. I am so sorry. And I am sorry that I was not there for you—your own bishop. Of course I forgive you. How can I not? So many times I have failed my wife, my friends . . . and God has forgiven me. We will talk no more about it. It is completely covered by the blood of Jesus."

Yacobo nodded, for a moment speechless in the big bear hug the bishop gave him. Now he was free.

As he turned to go, he said, "Oh, I almost forgot." Reaching into the pouch, he drew out a handful of papers, which he handed to the bishop. "This is something I've written—after not being able to write anything for almost two years. It is called 'Martyrs' Song,' the same title as the play. In fact, it covers some of the same stories as the other things I've written. But this time it is *my* testimony, how the deaths of the martyrs of Uganda, including the arch-bishop and my brother, Blasio, have helped me understand freedom in Christ."

The bishop took the manuscript. "Thank you, Yacobo. I will gladly read it." He laughed. "You will be published yet, young man!"

Yacobo grinned. "No, thank *you*, Bishop Kivengere. It was your little book, *I Love Idi Amin,* that showed me the power of a testimony—words on paper—to change people's lives."

More About Festo Kivengere

HE WAS BORN IN A TRADITIONAL "KRAAL" of the Bahima or cattle herders of the Bahororo tribe in Uganda, probably in 1919 or 1920. Kivengere, as he was named, was a grandson of the last great chief of the Bahororo tribe. But just before the turn of the century, Uganda had become a British protectorate that linked the various tribes into a coalition, using tribal chiefs as local government officials.

Formal education was primarily provided by "mission schools." At the age of eleven, Kivengere was designated a "reader" and eligible to receive Christian baptism. It was the custom for Christian godparents to choose a biblical name at baptism, so young Kivengere was christened "Festus" (or Festo) after the Roman governor in Acts.

His conversion was genuine in the sense that he left the religion of pagan spirits behind, but it was a conversion based on law, not grace, and by the time he went to university, he had become a cynical agnostic. At the age of nineteen, he was horrified to return to his hometown of Rukungiri and find newly converted Christians praising the Lord in the street, returning stolen goods, asking forgiveness of people they had wronged. This was sheer fanaticism!

The East African Revival, as it came to be known, swept across Kenya, Uganda, and other East African countries. His younger sister, his niece, even his best friend were all praying for Festo. Finally he fell to his knees and committed his life to following Jesus with his whole heart.

What a transformation! The sacrificial love of Jesus filled his heart and began to change him. He asked his abusive stepfather, whom he had hated for many years, to forgive him for his hatred. He was also convicted to ask the forgiveness of a white missionary whom he had resented and had spoken against behind his back. The words "Please forgive me" broke down walls of separation between these men and resulted in reconciliation. Festo was amazed at the power of Christ's revolutionary love.

Although trained as a teacher, his real passion became evangelism. In 1945, he and his wife, Mera, went as "missionary teachers" to Dodoma, Tanzania, where Festo spent every available weekend and holiday on preaching missions to the surrounding villages and towns. Their family was growing, and by the time they returned to Uganda in 1956, they had four girls: Peace, Joy, Hope, and Charity. But they left behind a little grave: Lydia, their second child, had died in Dodoma the same day Joy was born.

The reconciling love of Christ became a major theme in Festo's preaching. A dynamic preacher, he was invited to speak in Australia and Britain. He also translated for the American evangelist Billy Graham when he came to Africa in 1960, eventually giving up teaching for full-time evangelism both at home and abroad. Teaming up with South Africa's Michael Cassidy, Festo Kivengere helped the evangelistic and relief organization known as African Enterprise spread over many African countries, eventually reaching around the world.

Uganda, meanwhile, was marching toward independence from Britain, which she obtained in 1962. Kabaka, king of Baganda, the largest Ugandan province, became the president of this new independent nation, and Milton Obote was its prime minister. But in a swift military coup, Obote unseated Kabaka, who ended his days in exile in London. Less than ten years later, Obote's army chief of staff, Idi Amin, staged a military coup of his own and took over as "president for life."

Uganda, the "pearl of Africa," with its rich resources, mild climate, and fertile farmland, was rapidly being torn apart by tribal rivalries and civil war. Against this backdrop, Festo became ordained in the Anglican Church, then was appointed bishop of the Kigezi district in southwestern Uganda. His message of the reconciling love of Christ and forgiving one's enemies faced its greatest challenge during the reign of terror of the 1970s, when thousands of Ugandans died at the hands of Idi Amin's military rule.

After the death of Anglican Archbishop Janini Luwum, Festo and Mera fled for their lives. But Festo had to bring his hard and bitter attitude toward Amin to the foot of the Cross. "I had to ask for forgiveness from the Lord," he wrote, "and the grace to love President Amin more." The years in exile were fruitful ones, as Festo continued his evangelistic missions, pled the plight of Uganda before foreign governments, and established a relief organization to help resettled Ugandan refugees. But at the news that Idi Amin had been driven from Uganda, Festo canceled all his scheduled meetings and went home as quickly as possible. Uganda was hurting and needed the healing message of Christ's love.

Milton Obote returned and won a popular election but turned around and retaliated against the northern tribes that were considered loyal to Amin. Hundreds of thousands more died before he was overthrown by Yoweri Museveni at the end of 1985. Museveni is still president of a Uganda that is gradually reclaiming its stability and prosperity.

All through those years, Festo not only continued the work of African Enterprise and evangelistic tours around the world but was deeply concerned for the children of Uganda, who had grown up only knowing terror. He also started an immunization program against the numerous epidemics that were taking many lives, as well.

In 1988, Festo Kivengere succumbed to leukemia, but the "Billy Graham of Africa," as he was sometimes called, had touched the lives of millions with his message of revolutionary love.

For Further Reading

Coomes, Anne. *Festo Kivengere: A Biography*. Eastbourne, East Sussex: Monarch Publications, 1990.

Kivengere, Bishop Festo, with Dorothy Smoker. *Revolutionary Love*. Fort Washington, Penn.: Christian Literature Crusade, 1983.

Kivengere, Bishop Festo, with Dorothy Smoker. *I Love Idi Amin*. Old Tappan, N.J.: Fleming H. Revell Company, 1977. Subtitle: *The Story of Triumph Under Fire in the Midst of Suffering and Persecution in Uganda*.